"So we are cousins," observed Mr. Brand

"And it will be perfectly proper for me to live with you," Elinor asserted. "Although, of course, I shall have to have a chaperon."

"You seem to have arranged things to your satisfaction," he remarked, and Elinor blushed at his tone. "Is there anything else you wish to say before we part?"

"Part, sir? I'm afraid I cannot leave."

"Cannot leave?" Mr. Brand responded coldly. "Madam, you cannot stay!"

Helen May

**is also the author of
Masquerade #55**

Duel of Love

They called her the Crystal Venus....

She was Miss Cassandra Wells of
Ridgefield, independent lady, spinster by
choice. And behind her unyielding back
her London friends made her an object
of gossip.

Horrified at her nickname, Cassandra was
forced to take a second look at herself. Did
she really appear as cold and glacial as
crystal—and as hard? Just because she'd
made it clear she didn't want a lover...?

With a jolt she wondered if Lord Verax,
too, called her the Crystal Venus behind
her back.

She was surprised to discover that she
hoped he did not!

Chance of Love

HELEN MAY

A MASQUERADE FROM

W🌐RLDWIDE

TORONTO • LONDON • NEW YORK • SYDNEY

Masquerade edition published March 1982
ISBN 0-373-30085-9

Originally published in 1981
by Mills & Boon Limited

Printed in Canada

CHAPTER
ONE

At the age of eighteen years and eight months Miss Elinor Graham was certain of two things. One that she would make an indifferent school-ma'am; the other that the *ton* world was somewhere in which a determined young woman could find excitement and eventual financial security.

She explained her views yet again to Miss Brown, whose hands fluttered helplessly as she protested, 'But, my dearest Elinor, you cannot possibly be serious about following such a course of action. I am afraid it would be improper!'

At Elinor's indignant glance she amended, 'Well, unwise!' Her thin nose quivered in agitation.

Elinor seated herself by the school proprietress and gave her hand a kindly pat. 'I do know what you mean, dear Miss Brown, but I have thought it all out and know how to attain the position I desire. At least,' she conceded, 'I know how I shall make the attempt.'

'Oh, pray consider my offer, Elinor! With your own little income and a stipend as a teacher you will be well before with the world and free to take part in all the activities of our own small town. You are so pretty and clever you will be bound to meet some young man who . . .'

'. . . who will install me in a tiny house and make me mamma to a family of children who we will then endeavour to educate, feed and clothe with a minimum of wealth. I do not see my life like that at all.' She raised a slender hand. 'Do not argue any more, I beg. Some of my fondest memories have been fashioned here and I do not want to quarrel with you, but I cannot visualise myself as the wife of a country squireen. And as for teaching. . . !' Elinor gave a delicate shudder. 'You cannot have considered the idea carefully enough. I am not at all the sort of person you want.'

Elinor's large blue-grey eyes lighted as a smile curved her generous mouth. 'You see, you cannot deny that I am too wilful to become a schoolma'am. No, I shall pursue my goal, and when I am a rich and famous London hostess I shall ask you to stay with me as my honoured guest.'

Miss Brown made a last struggle. 'At least first *write* to Mr Jonas Webb. It would be too dreadful if he were to turn you away, though of course you are welcome to return here at any time, Elinor.'

'You are the soul of goodness, ma'am. As I have explained, I shall not write to Papa's cousin because he may tell me that he does not want me to visit him, but if I simply arrive on his doorstep I am convinced that I can persuade him to allow me to remain, at least until the end of the present Season. That is not long. Already it is June.'

Elinor rose, kissed her teacher's cheek, then walked swiftly out of the small sitting-room, up the stairs, and into her bedchamber.

Mention of Papa had overwhelmed her with her sense of loss. Only three months had passed since the letters had arrived, and it was with difficulty that she withheld her tears. But she would not give way to an emotion which her father had forbidden. A memory of his graceful figure, his warm smile, his sense of humour which she had inherited, brought a stiffening of her resolve. He would have approved of her plan. He could so easily have tied up her modest inheritance in a way which would have leaked small amounts to her at intervals, but in a grand gesture so native to him he had invested her with the power to spend the thousand pounds when and how she pleased. Now the money was available.

Elinor finished packing her trunk and bandbox. This would be her last night at Miss Brown's Academy for Young Ladies, and she had visualised her departure in so different a light. Now there would be no journey abroad in the charge of some lady traveller to rejoin her father at whatever residence he presently inhabited. For the first time in her life she tasted loneliness. Even when Papa had been many miles away the knowledge of his being in the world was enough to sustain her through their separation.

She had hated the idea of leaving him at all. From the time Mamma had left them he had kept her close to him and together they had laughed their way through Europe, the West Indies and America, sometimes living in high style, sometimes in a couple of dingy rooms, depending on whether or not Papa had been lucky at the gaming tables.

Elinor could only recall her mother as a pair of warm encircling arms and a sweet scent, and Papa always talked of her beauty and gaiety and never once reproached her for leaving him. 'I had not the right to wed her, Elinor,' he always said. 'She was so lovely, and deserved a better fate than the one I offered her. Yet I cannot regret everything because she gave you to me, little sweetheart. You're the only woman I shall ever want now.'

Once Elinor asked, 'Did not Mamma want to take me with her?'

His reply, 'Maybe she did, but her—friend would not have you—or perhaps she saw that I needed you,' had entirely satisfied her, and she had not asked again. And so they had travelled the world bound in love and laughter; they lived like princes, or they patched their clothes and ate bread and cheese. It mattered nothing to either of them, and Elinor had envisaged such a life for ever. Time seemed not to touch them until the day Papa had arrived home unexpectedly to find his sixteen-year-old daughter wrestling in the arms of a gaming acquaintance.

True, Elinor had just dented a copper vase over the upstart's head, but she had discovered then for the first time that Papa could be exceedingly angry and she had watched with amazement as her father had waded into a bout of fisticuffs and floored his opponent in minutes.

As the discomfited man fled, holding a cloth to his streaming nose and rapidly blackening eye, Elinor clasped her hands. 'Famous, Papa! I did not know you could fight!'

'At Eton I learned more than Latin and Greek,' said her father, but he was surprisingly serious as he asked, 'How old are you, sweeting?'

'I shall be seventeen quite soon, Papa.'

'Seventeen! Where have the years gone? You are almost a woman!'

Elinor had been gratified, but her pleasure had turned to bewilderment a few weeks later when he told her in tones that brooked no argument that she was to go to school in England and that, being in funds, he had secured a sum of money which would keep her there for two years.

'I have been selfish,' he said. 'You are well-born, Elinor, and I have not given you the opportunity to acquire the feminine accomplishments due to your station.'

Elinor lifted her pillow and took up a page of her father's last letter which was crumpled from her constant perusal and her early tears. It had been posted in Florence and was dated February, 1819.

'. . . when you read these words, my little sweeting, I shall have left this world. My deepest regret lies in not seeing you one last time. I have known for some months that I was to die, but I did not wish to come to you with pockets to let. My luck was right out. Then I put all I could raise on the turn of a card and, my darling, I won! One thousand pounds! I meant to bring it to you, but the medical men say I shall not arrive in time, so I am sending the money with one I trust, to be held for you by our old family man of business. May God be with you . . .'

Elinor read it again before placing it in her reticule with the letter from the lawyer who had mixed his expressions of commiseration with platitudes regarding the irregular life led, and lost, by one so youthful, along with advice about placing her funds in a secure trust which would bring her a small income.

Elinor set her lips as she pulled the straps of her trunk tight then smiled at the maid who knocked and entered. 'Have you come to say goodbye, Nancy? I regret having to leave you.'

'Then don't, Miss Elinor. Let me come with you. How can you manage all alone?'

'But I shall not be "all alone". I shall be with a cousin of Papa's. And I cannot possibly afford a servant. By the time I have purchased a minimum of fashionable gowns and some small pieces of inexpensive jewellery I shall have to live very economically.'

'I would work for no wages if you'd take me. Oh, I'd just love to see you mixing with the gentry coves! I don't blame you for taking your chances.'

Elinor raised her well-defined dark brows. 'Do you not, Nancy? Miss Brown is scandalised. She is also shocked that I am not going into deepest mourning for my father, but he requested that I should not.' Elinor gave a twisted smile. 'How he would laugh to know that I was going to risk my entire legacy on a fling at the London Season! *He* would comprehend that the idea of passing my life in genteel poverty appals me.'

'*I* understand, Miss Elinor. Say you'll take me.'

'I thought you had a good place here.'

'Well, it's better than some, though I get sick of Cook always screeching and giving me clouts. And besides, I'd like to be a lady's-maid.'

Elinor looked quickly at Nancy's short, dumpy figure and thick fingers. 'Don't throw away a secure post for a chancy life with me, my dear. I may fail.' At Nancy's disbelieving exclamation she added, 'Well, I do not contemplate it, but if I did, what would become of you? When I am ensconced in my rich home I will send for you to be trained as an upper housemaid. Who knows, you may end as my housekeeper.'

Nancy shook her head dolefully and Elinor finished her preparations and composed herself to sleep, and at dawn on a fine summer morning she followed her luggage pushed in a barrow by the school porter to join a stage-coach bound for London.

When the stage pulled to a halt Elinor stood back politely to allow a bent, heavily swathed figure to precede her. The woman was not on the bill, and Elinor saw money change hands. The unforeseen passenger meant that the other travellers were squeezed together in an uncomfortable manner, and Elinor wrinkled her nostrils at the odours of damp shoe leather and straw, stale perfume, tobacco and onions which pervaded the coach, while she ignored the nods and leers of a young man in a moleskin jacket who sat opposite.

As the stage rumbled over a particularly bumpy stretch of road he allowed himself to be jolted in a manner which led to his placing a hand on Elinor's knee in a spurious attempt to regain his balance, and Elinor was amazed to see the still-swathed figure of the bent lady leap into sudden life as a fleshy hand emerged from the cloak to slap the man, while a well-remembered voice cried, 'Leave my young mistress be!'

Elinor sighed. 'All right, Nancy, you can remove your disguise. What Miss Brown will say when you return. . . !'

'Shan't be going back,' said Nancy briefly, 'and

she won't mind, on account of she's as worried about you as I am, so there! Anyway I've used all my money on the ticket and the extra to bribe the guard.'

The man in the moleskin jacket became articulate. 'Jest who d'you think you're a-knockin' about?'

A fat farming wife with a large basket on her knees joined in. 'She be thumpin' you, that's who, and if you was to ask me, someone ought to tell the guard at the next postin' house that you be tryin' to molest us women, and he'll put you off the coach.'

'I never laid a finger on you!'

'Ah, but there's no tellin' what you'll do next. I seen you touch that young lady there. We all did, didn't we?'

Nods and murmurs of assent from the other passengers drove the abashed man to subside with incoherent mutters, and Elinor decided to leave the matter of the truant Nancy until they were alone.

But at the posting house in Kingston where everybody dashed into the Castle Inn for ale to wash the dust of summer from parched throats Nancy refused to be moved by Elinor's arguments. And when they arrived in London as the church clocks were striking eleven in the morning, Elinor was glad to have Nancy with her.

They journeyed in a hackney to Upper Brook Street and stood together at the front door of a small but well-designed house.

'Door needs painting,' murmured Nancy, as Elinor rapped the knocker.

A footman appeared, still fastening the buttons of his waistcoat. He stared at the women. 'We don't want whatever you're selling,' he said, before he met Elinor's eyes. 'B . . . beg your pardon, ma'am. Well, how was I to know . . . Ladies with no escorts at an unmarried gentleman's door . . .'

'Be so good,' intoned Elinor, in compelling accents, 'as to step aside and allow us to enter. I am not accustomed to stand waiting upon doorsteps.'

The footman's mouth fell open and he hastily regained his manners and showed them into the hall.

'Kindly inform your master that we would like to see him,' said Elinor.

'M . . . my m . . . master? B . . . but he's still abed!'

Elinor had not moved in gaming circles without acquiring a sound education in the ways of men. 'Up till all hours, I daresay. We will wait.'

She looked about her. 'I expect that if you gave the matter thought you could conduct us to a more suitable place,' she suggested.

'Oh! Ah! Please come this way.'

Elinor and Nancy looked about them in the small ground-floor drawing-room, and Nancy marched to the window to draw the curtains. Sunshine flooded in and illumined a room which clearly had been at its best many years before. The upholstery was worn and even holed in places, and Nancy drew a finger along the top of a drum table and frowned. 'Dust! And lots of it! What kind of man is this cousin of your father's, Miss Elinor?'

'Maybe we should not judge him harshly,' replied Elinor, brushing a giltwood sofa with her handkerchief before seating herself. 'Mr Jonas Webb is elderly. He may be an invalid. Perhaps he is failing in sight. He is being exploited by careless servants, that is certain. I thought at first he had been card-playing till daybreak, but now I question if he leaves his bed often. I wonder if I should call the footman and suggest we visit Papa's cousin in his bedchamber? It could not be considered improper in such a case.'

Her musings were halted by the sound of footsteps, and her heartbeat quickened at the opening of the drawing-room door.

A tall man entered and immediately covered his eyes. 'Who in heaven's name pulled the curtains back? I am almost blinded. Oh, my head! Thomas! Fetch brandy—at once!'

This was something Elinor understood. She spoke severely. 'Coffee, preferably black, or soda water, would do you infinitely more good than brandy.'

The man peered through the dusty shafts of sunlight. 'I do not know you, madam, and cannot conceive of your reason for being here, but this is my house and if I choose to drink brandy in it I shall most certainly do so.'

'Your house?'

'Mine!'

Elinor looked at Nancy. 'Have we arrived at the wrong place? Oh, I do hope so, for this state of dilapidation is not at all what I hoped for. Is this not the residence of Mr Jonas Webb, sir? I know you cannot be he, for I discovered that his age is at least seventy years and you cannot be much above thirty—though your mode of life does not flatter your looks,' she added sternly.

The man gave a sardonic bow, winced and raised

long white fingers to his brow before he turned to tug the bell-pull at the fireplace. 'That is a piece of information I require from no one, not even my friends, of which you, madam, are not one. Ah, Thomas,' he said to the footman who had appeared with a tray carrying brandy and a glass, 'these— er—young ladies have clearly strayed into the wrong house. Be so good as to show them to the door.'

'Do nothing of the kind, please, Thomas,' said Elinor. 'I wish to speak further to your master.'

Thomas looked hesitantly at the man who waved him out before saying faintly, 'Pray sit down, if you must stay.' He then subsided into an easy chair, arranged his ankle-length burgundy red dressing-gown around him, and downed a glass of brandy.

Elinor smiled at Nancy. 'Go and find the kitchen, dear, and procure some refreshment. I am sure you need it.'

Nancy hesitated, then left, and Elinor gave her attention to the man who said, 'Now, perhaps you will inform me of your reason for forcing me from my bed little more than six hours after I climbed into it. When Thomas told me of females in the drawing-room I thought . . .' He seemed to recollect himself. 'Well, no matter.' He poured himself a smaller measure of brandy and viewed Elinor. 'Please be as brief as possible. I want only to return to bed.'

'What a way to live! My name is Elinor Graham, and my maid is Nancy Wood. We have come to join the household of Mr Webb. He is my only surviving relative—at least, he is the only one who seems likely to help me. If you will be good enough to direct me to him, I shall trouble you no further.'

'That will not be easy, Miss Graham. I regret to have to tell you that Mr Webb left this vale of tears some two months since. Furthermore, he was *my* relative, and I have no recollection of a Miss Elinor Graham in my family.'

'Oh! Well, I am sorry to learn of Cousin Jonas's death, though I must be honest and say that since we had never met I am probably sorrier for myself than for him. I was depending on using this address as a base for my activities in London.'

'Which are—or rather were?'

'To clothe myself as well as possible on one thousand pounds and use what is left of the Season to meet the right kind of people.'

'Are you sure who they are?'

A gleam of humour lit the man's dark eyes and a sardonic smile fleetingly touched his face. For the first time Elinor noted that he was attractive in a thin, saturnine way. He continued to gaze at her and she felt nervous as she replied.

'I am not sure of anything at present, sir.' Briefly she told him what had occurred to her and finished, 'So you see why I must move quickly if I am not to waste my subsistence. Already I am nearly nineteen, which is considered, I believe, quite old to make a come-out.'

The man poured himself another glass of brandy. His dissipated life-style seemed not to have affected him unduly, and his shapely white hands were steady. He leaned back and gave Elinor a searching stare and she felt positive that he knew to a penny how little her garments had cost.

'Might I point out,' he enquired in tones of disarming softness, 'that the Season has but seven or eight weeks to run? In fact several of our most fashionable hostesses are preparing already to abandon London because of the excessive heat of this summer.'

Elinor set her lips. 'I am not unaware of the necessity to make haste, sir, but my money will not last long. I must use it to the best advantage.'

'Go back to school, Miss Graham. Your teacher's advice is exactly what I would give you.' He yawned behind his hand. 'I am sorry you have had your journey for nothing.'

Elinor's eyes sparked. 'So far, sir, you have given me no clue to your identity! I should like to know the name of the man to whom I am indebted for such unwarranted and unwanted instructions.'

The man's eyes travelled slowly from her plain bonnet to her serviceable shoes and back again. Then he rose, gave a bow which appeared to cause him further distress, before he subsided once more into his chair. 'Christopher Brand, ma'am, the owner of this house.'

'Oh, so that is who you are!' Elinor was relieved. 'Papa used to talk of our family and tell me where they might be found. Mr Jonas Webb, was your uncle—your mother's brother, who was second cousin to my father.'

Mr Brand looked dazed. 'Was he?' he asked, encompassing all the men in one phrase. 'Well, Miss Elinor Graham, I have been frank with you, but I have still to know if you are indeed a relative. Not, I hasten to add, that I will admit a claim to protection of any young woman, but especially one of whom I have never before heard.'

Elinor opened her reticule and produced a small sheaf of papers which she handed in silence to Mr Brand. He read them rapidly, then returned them.

'They are quite in order,' he confessed, and Elinor caught the hint of regret in his tone. 'It seems we are distant cousins.'

'So it will be perfectly proper for me to remain beneath your roof,' asserted Elinor. She ignored the narrowing of his eyes and asked, 'Pray, will you not tell me how old you are?'

His brows climbed. 'I am two and thirty, and will not for one moment consider . . .'

'Almost as old as my dear papa when he . . . left me. He was but nine and thirty. He and Mamma were married almost out of the schoolroom.'

Mr Brand's voice was unexpectedly gentle. 'Miss Graham, I am paying you the compliment of believing you to be as aware as I am that a distant bachelor cousin of two and thirty is as far removed from a guardian papa of any age as is oil from water.'

A flush ran under Elinor's delicate skin as Mr Brand continued to gaze at her. He was disturbingly attractive, and she wondered for a moment what he thought of her. Her face held more character than beauty and her hair could only be described as fair, but her eyes were large and long-lashed, her complexion flawless and her figure excellent.

'Of course I could not stay here without chaperonage,' she conceded.

Mr Brand looked triumphant. 'I entirely agree.'

'Therefore it will be necessary to send for some elderly female, preferably indigent, for then she will be eager to come.'

She had begun with bravado which faded beneath Mr Brand's cool sarcasm as he answered, 'I feel convinced that you know of such a female among our mutual relatives.'

'There is Miss Tabitha Claypole in Blackburn. That is a northern town which has become devoted to industry, so I daresay she would be glad to leave it.'

Mr Brand's long fingers slowly tapped the arm of his chair. 'I must conclude that your recent incarceration in the schoolroom has given you the desire to impart knowledge. Thank you for the geography lesson!' He held up a hand as Elinor began to retort. 'So you really think to bring me another mouth to feed?'

'No I do not, sir! Naturally I will contribute my share to the expenses of the household and pay extra for my companion.'

'And your maid?'

'Of course her wage will be my responsibility.'

'You appear to have arranged things to your own satisfaction.'

Elinor clenched her fists. 'Surely it can mean nothing to you to let me remain here for a short time, and it could alter the entire shape of my life.' She looked around her. 'N . . . no doubt you will use your own money to put this place in order. One can scarcely give entertainments . . .'

Her voice trailed off as Mr Brand began to shake his head in a most irritating manner. 'I will outline my position to you, Miss Graham, after which you will see that the sooner you take yourself and your thousand pounds away the better it will be for you. I daresay you have come to London in the mistaken belief that its pavements are lined with gold.'

'Do not be absurd, sir,' flashed Elinor. 'I am not such an ignoramus.'

Black brows drew together above the penetrating dark eyes. 'I rejoice to hear it. Yet you assume that I am possessed of wealth sufficient to set to rights this decaying residence. Allow me to enlighten you, madam. I have an income which is moderate, but sufficient for my needs. I usually reside in comfortable bachelor quarters which I have given up to attend to the disposal of my late uncle's so-called assets. I employ an excellent valet who, with some landlady to clean and cook, is the only domestic I require. I have been left with this broken-down encumbrance and not a penny with which to run it, and the sooner I can sell it the happier I shall be.'

'Surely this is not all that your uncle left! Papa said he was a man of substance.'

'*Was*, Miss Graham. Unfortunately he was also a gambler. He spent his declining years in entertaining a few old cronies, drinking as much as possible and throwing his possessions at the servants. My bedchamber, which was his, was littered with bits of pottery and glass.'

'How perfectly dreadful! I begin to see that he was not the kind of man with whom I would have wished to reside. And is this your entire inheritance?'

'No, there is also the matter of a manor house in Gloucestershire.'

Elinor's eyes sparkled. 'There must be income from that!'

'Not so, I fear. I had my lawyer examine the property and he says it is in a far worse state than the London residence. Apparently my uncle had not visited it in years. Rents are owing from farms and cottages, and there is no hope of regaining these moneys from the poverty-stricken tenants.'

'But that is shameful!' declared Elinor.

'I do so agree with you, ma'am.'

'It is clear to me that Mr Jonas Webb must have neglected his obligations in a shocking way, and that the tenants saw no reason why they should pay rents to a man who cared not a fig for them.'

Mr Brand looked astonished. 'I confess I had not considered that aspect.'

'But you should, sir! These are your people now. You owe it to them to discover their needs. What if some other unscrupulous person were to buy the estate and turn them all from their homes?'

Mr Brand contemplated the vision conjured by Elinor of a small army of men, women and children thrown summarily on to the roads. He regarded her from beneath his lids. 'You appear to have a re-markable talent for attributing bad behaviour to me. I will advise my lawyer to sell to a humane person. Will that do?'

Elinor answered spiritedly, 'It would not do for me, sir!'

'Indeed! Well, madam, I have not your crusading spirit. And furthermore, Miss Graham, I have not your talent for invading the privacy of someone's life and giving them unasked-for advice on how to conduct it.'

'I should not have dreamed of coming here had I known *you* were in possession,' cried Elinor.

'I am relieved to hear it. Tell me, as a matter of interest, if you have spent your life roaming the world's capitals, how can you claim to know so much about farmers and peasants?'

'Britain is not the only place where rural populations are exploited by absentee landlords, sir!'

Mr Brand regarded her coldly. 'I am learning much this morning. I am ruining my health by living a life of dissipation. I am careless of the needs of others, and I am a ruthless absentee landlord.' He laid down his glass and stretched. 'God, I am weary! I shall return to my rest. Is there any other particular part of my character you care to demolish before we part?'

CHAPTER
TWO

His tone was dismissive, and Elinor coloured. 'I apologise if I have been too direct. As for leaving—that I cannot do.'

Mr Brand had begun to rise, but sank back now with a look of amazement. 'I beg your pardon? Cannot leave? Madam, you cannot stay and there's an end to the matter!'

'Would you have me roam the London streets?'

'Good God, no! Cannot you go to some other relative? With your extensive knowledge of our family tree you must be able to call someone to mind. Female this time, I suggest.'

'You are set upon making me appear foolish. You are aware of the fact that I assumed I was coming to an elderly man.'

Mr Brand's lips twisted a little. 'You continue to prove how unfitted you are to be let loose in London. Some of our sorriest rake-hells are men whose years should have taught them moderation.'

'You sound remarkably like Miss Brown!'

'An admirable woman, evidently. But we digress. Whom do you know who could offer you sanctuary?'

'In London there is only Lady Smithson. She is the widow of the first cousin of my mamma.'

Mr Brand looked relieved. 'Capital! Just the thing! Only acquaint me with her direction and I will have the footman call a hackney and take you there. In fact, I will do more. I will dress and escort you myself.'

'What sacrifices you are prepared to make on my behalf,' said Elinor coldly, 'but it is not capital at all, sir. Lady Smithson has five daughters, three of whom are of marriageable age and two who must be considered left on the shelf, though I daresay they do not see it in that light.'

'Afraid of competition in the marriage mart?' said Mr Brand in scathing accents.

'I am afraid of nothing so trivial, sir. In any case, although I know I am not a beauty, from all I have heard, I have a modest advantage over them in looks and would be considered an unwelcome rival. But besides . . .'

She stopped and looked into the discouraging face of her cousin.

'Yes, Miss Graham?' he asked in anything but friendly tones.

'Besides,' said Elinor slowly, looking down at her hands, which showed a sudden tremor, 'Lady Smithson would most likely refuse me admittance, because Mamma did not die, as you possibly supposed, but ran away with a rich Earl and has not been heard of since—at least, not by me—and I am considered not quite—respectable. In fact it has been a source of worry to me that I may find it rather . . . difficult . . . to enter the *ton* world at all.'

She was unable to meet the gaze she knew he was directing at her. With the weapon she had handed him he could strike her ambitions a devastating blow. Why had she given him the lever with which he could so easily prise her from his house?

When he spoke again his voice was unexpectedly kind. 'She would hold your Mamma's behaviour against you?'

'Her letters to Papa at the time gave no room for doubt. When Papa—died—I was sent his personal papers. The letters were amongst them. They were—cruel.'

The silence continued for so long that Elinor forced herself to look up. Mr Brand was directing a ferocious frown upon her and when he spoke he sounded angry, though she felt that this time his emotion was not aimed at her. Finally he said, 'Well, you may stay here tonight—I will lodge with a friend.'

'Oh, thank you, sir!'

'But do not make any mistake. Tomorrow you will leave. Go back to your Miss Brown. Save your money and use it as a dowry.'

Elinor's temper flared. 'That I will not do! I do not yet know how it can be contrived, but I *will* stay in London.'

Mr Brand rose abruptly and a spasm of pain crossed his face. Elinor found it difficult to maintain her gaze as he asked, 'Have you always been so stubborn and wilful?'

'Is it stubborn to know what is best for oneself? Do you see me as a schoolma'am or governess? What other occupation is open to a lady?'

'Madam, I do not desire to quarrel with anyone this morning, least of all a female! As for your prospective occupation, I have never given the employment of women any thought.'

Elinor sprang to her feet and stared into the face which glowered above her. 'Exactly, sir. And until men do think lucidly about women we shall be forced into the only roads open to us, and I see none before me, except marriage to a man who can afford to allow me a measure of independence.'

'Well! You have an odd idea of marriage.'

'That remains to be seen. Have you any other suggestion for my future?'

He held a hand to his head and ruffled his Brutus haircut distractedly. 'How did I become involved in this? There I was, calmly sleeping off last night's wine, and suddenly I am accused of any manner of unpleasant things and, furthermore, asked to give consideration to the protection of a female relative.'

'I . . . I am sorry,' said Elinor.

'Sorry! If that were true you would instantly leave and go back to school. In fact, if you had a grain of common sense you would not have embarked on this ridiculous adventure at all.'

He peered into her face. 'You are not going to weep, are you? A typical female weapon!'

'I *never* weep, sir, unless it be absolutely necessary.'

He continued to observe her closely, and again a flush deepened her cheeks to rose. She heard his breath catch in his throat, then he said, almost to himself, 'I think perhaps Lady Smithson and her five daughters might find you a formidable obstacle in their pursuit of husbands.'

For an instant the barriers of antagonism were lowered and abruptly Elinor became aware of his masculinity, of the tautness of his lean body in the tightly-corded dressing-gown. The onslaught on her senses was so totally unexpected that she took a step back in trepidation.

Mr Brand turned from her and walked to the window out of which he stared for a moment before he turned. 'Miss Graham, you must believe me when I tell you that for your own safety you should go back to your Miss Brown. Do as she suggested and wait for a nice young man to come along and court you. Never fear, Miss Graham, there will always be someone.'

Elinor wanted to say something unanswerably scathing, but she could not find the words. Then he said, 'Well, we will let tomorrow take care of itself. Tonight you are in London. Would you care to visit the theatre?'

Her worries were put aside in her surprised acceptance, and she was shown upstairs to a room which was less dilapidated than the rest of the house, possibly from lack of use, and Nancy and the footman were bringing hot bricks to air the bed, and coal and sticks. Her cousin sent a message to say that he must go out, but would return for dinner.

Nancy helped Elinor to bathe in a tub before the fire and to dress. She chattered on about the state of the kitchen and the sluttishness of the cook as Elinor surveyed herself in a cheval-glass. She was not dissatisfied with her appearance. Her fair hair, brushed to a shine by Nancy, and her perfect skin were set off to advantage by her quiet gown of dove-grey muslin with lilac trimming, and the pearls round her throat and in her ears. In an oddly moral way, in view of her desertion, Mamma had left them behind for her daughter, and no matter how straitened their circumstances had been, Papa had never sold them.

She touched her jewels gently. Pearls were suitable for mourning. Strictly speaking she should not go into society, but phrases from her father's last letter came to mind, '. . . don't waste energy in useless grief, my Elinor. Use every moment of your time . . .'

She drew a white worsted shawl about her shoulders and descended to the living-room, where it took several seconds to recognise the elegant man in cream kerseymere breeches and a black coat with a gold chain across his waistcoat as Mr Brand. Two ladies were with him, and she curtseyed as Mr Brand said, 'Miss Graham, allow me to present you to Lady Sophia Deane and her aunt and companion, Mrs Jameson.'

Lady Sophia, who was about five and twenty, gave a cool smile. 'How charming! And so this child is your cousin. Well, I do see that you cannot remain here tonight without proper chaperonage.' She turned to Elinor. 'I was much diverted by the account of your precipitous flight from school!' Before Elinor could frame a suitable reply her ladyship spoke again to Mr Brand. 'If you would care for it I could take Miss Graham home as my guest.'

Elinor held her breath. Lady Sophia was exceedingly pretty, gowned in high fashion and on the surface, friendly, but instinctively she distrusted her and was relieved when Mr Brand declined the offer with many thanks and the assertion that he would not dream of putting her to such trouble for one night only.

During dinner it became apparent that Lady Sophia was a widow, that she was rich, and that she aspired to become the wife of Mr Brand. It was Elinor's opinion that a man who had managed to elude female capture for so many years was not a marrying man, but Lady Sophia allowed hints to drop in Elinor's direction that she would brook no rivals.

The atmosphere of *Romeo and Juliet* suited Elinor's melancholy mood, and afterwards she sat quietly through the farce—in which Lady Sophia and Mrs Jameson found much amusement— allowing Mr Brand, who cast several concerned glances her way, to assume that the risqué lines were beyond her comprehension, though she had lived too much in a very mixed society to be un-aware of much of their meaning.

That night she retired to bed with her head abuzz with impressions and speculations. Her cousin had seen her home, and after assuring himself that she would be supplied with supper, had gone to stay with an hospitable friend.

Elinor knew that he was as determined to see her depart on the morrow as she was to remain. She had no idea how she would contrive to manage the situation, but this house, shabby though it was, appeared to her to be her only hope of entering society, and somehow she must persuade Mr Brand that her plans were feasible.

She could not sleep. Images recurred in a tanta-lising manner. Scenes from the theatre; recol-lections from the past, and often and unwanted, the memory of a muscular male frame and mocking dark eyes. Her cousin was set on rejecting her and

Elinor tried to bring a calm contemplation to ways
to conquer his resolve, but always she was brought
back to the moment that morning when she had
become physically aware of him as a man.

She must contrive to hide any such emotion from
him. One hint that she could feel more for him than
a cousinly regard, and her chance of his protection
would dissolve like sugar in hot coffee.

Finally she drifted into sleep and rose later than
customary after a light breakfast carried up by
Nancy. Mr Brand was in the library and responded
to her curtsey with a bow. 'Have you packed? I will
escort you and your maid to the stage.'

'I have not,' said Elinor. She picked up a leather-
bound book and laid it down again. She glanced
around her at the almost empty shelves. 'I suppose
Mr Webb sold all the volumes of value.'

Mr Brand answered with another bow. 'You will
not wish to miss the stage. Shall I send upstairs for
your boxes?'

He looked elegant in a day coat, and trousers
strapped beneath his shoes, and Elinor had to force
herself to speak firmly. 'You must rid yourself of
this notion that I intend to return to school. I am
sure if we sat down and discussed the matter, we
could arrive at an arrangement which would suit us
both.'

'No, Miss Graham, it will not answer.'

She stared angrily at his set jaw. 'And is that your
final word?'

'It is.'

'Then, sir, you leave me with no alternative but
to cast myself on the mercy of the odious Lady
Smithson and her five daughters.'

She waited, but there was no response and she continued sadly, 'No, I could not bear it. She would criticise my parents, I would retaliate and we would be at odds immediately, even supposing she would admit me at all. I daresay Miss Tabitha Claypole will come to London and we can take lodgings. My thousand pounds should see me through the rest of the Season, and who knows, some gallant gentleman may be overcome by my charms.'

Mr Brand said harshly, 'Have no doubt of that, madam.'

She had to fight to control her voice. 'I suppose you will not object to introducing me to people? It could not be considered indiscreet for my closest male relative to do so. I am sure the gossips will come to terms with your refusal to allow me to remain respectably beneath your roof.'

'Have a care, madam. You are a reckless, scheming minx and may discover that you are no match for the society to which you aspire.'

'I am not unaware of my inexperience, cousin, which is why I came here for aid.'

'Aid is something I cannot offer,' returned Mr Brand. 'I am sorry for your predicament, truly I am, but you must go back to Miss Brown. Now, please ask your maid to pack quickly. There is still time to catch the coach.'

Elinor just managed to refrain from stamping her foot. She had an inclination to take her cousin by his fashionable double-breasted coat lapels and shake him. Only a brief contemplation of such a course was needed to persuade her that she did not dare.

'I will pack,' she said distantly, 'and I will stay in

London. You will not prevent me, sir. Indeed, you have no power to do so. I can only hope that your conscience will stir you into being prepared to vouch for me in society. I should think that your acquaintances might think it odd of you to refuse me so small a request.'

He turned his dark gaze on her and she compelled herself to meet it as he rasped, 'You are trying to gain your way by very devious means, madam. And I tell you here and now that you may do and say what you please. My reputation is secure enough, I warrant.'

Elinor's anger burst forth. 'I daresay you would much prefer it if I crept quietly into some establishment as a meek governess!'

'The idea of you as a meek anything—least of all a governess—is impossible to imagine. You, madam, are an overbearing, self-willed *female*. In fact, it is difficult to comprehend that you have just spent two years in an academy for young ladies.'

'Do not forget the years with a papa who was charming, loving and clever enough to keep us fed and happy by using his wits.'

Elinor had meant to maintain her air of authority, but the sudden aching memories conjured by her words caused her voice to break and, to her horror, large tears formed in her eyes and rolled slowly down her cheeks. She willed herself not to cry; she wanted to speak, but her throat was constricted. She waited for Mr Brand's further barbs as she recalled that she had informed him that she wept only when necessary.

He did not speak. Instead he bowed, handed her a large handkerchief, and walked to the window, gazing out into the street until she had sufficient time to regain her composure.

When she turned to face him again he said in a voice so unexpectedly gentle that her emotions were threatened again, 'I did not mean to upset you, cousin.'

'I . . . I beg your pardon for betraying such weakness, especially to a stranger.'

He gave a reluctant smile. 'You have spirit! I like that. And I see you are determined to remain in town. No, hear me out. I do not approve, but it is obvious to me that, in spite of your sojourn abroad and your unconventional life, you are as unfitted to pit your wits against London society as a babe. God help me, but I cannot see a young girl, a relative moreover, thrown to the wolves. I think I have run mad, but you may send for your Miss Claypole and stay here, at least until I dispose of the house.'

At this sudden capitulation Elinor forgot herself. 'Oh, how immensely kind you are!' She put out her arms as if to embrace him, then recollected herself and clasped her hands instead. Her face was alight with her gratitude and relief and her cousin caught his breath.

'There are times when you are more than pretty, Elinor.' Then he added, 'I shall stay with my friend until the arrival of Miss Claypole.'

Elinor felt suddenly awkward. 'Am I to call you "Christopher"? You have used my name.'

Mr Brand's lips twisted a little. 'No, my child, you may not. I shall remain at the proper distance which befits a guardian.'

She swept him a low curtsey and glanced up at

him through her curling dark lashes. 'Why, thank you, sir.'

Mr Brand grinned wolfishly. 'No, you are not exactly pretty, Elinor, but you have something more than mere looks. I shall derive amusement in watching the men tumble over themselves for your favours, though never forget that although it is the fashion to pay extravagant compliments, there are few who will offer marriage to a girl without a fortune.'

'I am grateful for the warning, *Cousin* Christopher. And now may I go to the shops and warehouses? I need some new gowns and gloves and things.'

Her cousin shrugged. 'Do as you will. I wonder how your father ever persuaded you to leave him and seek an education.'

Elinor said softly, 'His wish was always first with me. His loving care for me could not be surpassed, nor mine for him.'

'Then allow me to stand in his place and tell you something he undoubtedly would have known, which is that no lady goes shopping before the noon hour. No fashionable lady, I should say.'

'Then naturally I shall not,' conceded Elinor and retired to pen a letter to Miss Claypole.

She dismissed the hackney in Oxford Street and, attended by Nancy, was about to enter a muslin warehouse when a landau drawn by a pair of matched greys was pulled to a halt by the liveried coachman and Lady Sophia waited for her footman to lower the steps before she descended, followed by her faithful companion. Her appearance was so well-timed that Elinor wondered briefly if she was being spied upon.

'How are you, Miss Graham?' asked her ladyship, then without waiting for an answer enquired, 'Are you about to sample the delights of purchasing material? By a coincidence I also am in pursuit of muslin. Such a hot summer we are having, are we not? I declare one cannot have too many gowns.'

Elinor's mind travelled briefly over the half-dozen dresses in her well-worn wardrobe as she assented, and they entered the warehouse. She was bemused by the sight of the many bolts of material and dazzled by the colours and designs. Lady Sophia bought with wealthy abandon and the black-clad purveyors bowed low in their appreciation.

Then Elinor was swept by her ladyship from modiste to bonnet maker; from collections of reticules and gloves to fans, stockings and lace manufactories. Lady Sophia purchased with almost profligate carelessness. Nothing so vulgar as money was mentioned, but Elinor was able to realise that she must exercise great care if her thousand pounds was not to melt.

Within days Miss Tabitha Claypole presented herself at the Upper Brook Street house. She was exceedingly thin, of medium height with eyes of mid-brown, and lack-lustre hair spattered with grey. She wore a shabby gown and a black cloak shiny from use, and her skin was of a disturbing pallor. She brought few possessions, and Elinor realised that if Miss Claypole was to escort her into society she would need to buy garments for her also. Miss Claypole's manner was self-effacing, and judicious questioning elicited the facts that, after many years of service as a governess, she was now unable to obtain employment because of the weakened state of her lungs and had retired to her birthplace, a tiny house in Blackburn.

'It was used to be quite countrified,' she said in her breathless voice, 'but it has been overtaken by industry. There is smoke and grime everywhere.'

As if to emphasise the truth of her words she was shaken by a fit of coughing, and her resultant weakness and damp upper lip hinted strongly at a lack of nutrition as well as broken health.

Mr Brand moved back into the house and Elinor wished she could turn to him for advice, since it was obvious that Miss Tabitha could neither be turned away nor, in her present condition, accompany Elinor on the extensive round of parties she planned. She was deterred from approaching her cousin by the sardonic gleam in his eye which proclaimed that he was aware of her dilemma and found it diverting. Yet he surprised Elinor by the gentle probing of his talks with Miss Tabitha, by which he confirmed that her income was minute and that for some time past her diet had been inadequate. He then combined with Elinor in a wordless conspiracy to encourage the former governess to eat as much nourishing food as possible. In return Miss Tabitha offered to sew for Elinor and assured her that she could fashion gowns and bonnets with professional skill.

Lady Sophia called several times and after she learned that Mr Brand was permitting his cousin to

remain in his house her smiles grew less gracious
and her manner somewhat abrasive.

She was sitting with Elinor, Mrs Jameson and Mr
Brand in the drawing-room which had been rendered less dusty by Nancy's vigorous efforts when
the footman brought Mr Brand a letter. He excused
himself and opened it, his forehead creasing as he
read.

'Not bad news, I trust,' said Elinor gently.

He shook his head, folding the letter and putting
it into his pocket. 'Not exactly—something which
gives me concern, that is all.' He then returned to
the discussion of which party would be best to use
for Elinor's launching into society. As if I were a
ship, thought Elinor, though she could not afford
to be other than grateful to her ladyship who, as
well as offering much advice, was prepared to
chaperone her until such time as Miss Tabitha felt
well.

'You are fortunate, Elinor,' Mr Brand said later
that day. 'Lady Sophia is accepted everywhere. I
have never known her undertake such a mission
before.'

Elinor almost glared at him. Even the cleverest of
men could be dull-witted, she thought, when a
woman was managing him. It was perfectly obvious
to her that Lady Sophia would marry her off as fast
as possible to the highest bidder, so that she could
be removed from daily contact with the man she
herself coveted. The idea gave her a sharp pang in
her breast, and she was thankful to be able to
change the subject as her cousin brought his letter
out to read again.

He looked so solemn that Elinor asked, 'Are you

sure you have not had bad news? I would be glad to help you, if I could.'

'Thank you Elinor. This letter does give me concern. It is from Sir Henry Barnwall, a magistrate who resides near the Gloucestershire property. He says that a travelling man—a gipsy—was found dead inside the boundary wall of my estate. It seems that someone was surprised by a gamekeeper in the act of removing the body, and dropped it and fled. It is suggested that the gipsy was poaching.'

Elinor said slowly, 'People in Britain are poor and hungry, are they not? I suppose he was after some food for his family.'

Her cousin frowned. 'I trust you do not suppose my concern lies with a hungry wretch poaching a rabbit or pheasant.'

'I do not think you so unkind,' protested Elinor, anxious to restore the amity of the past days, which had been unexpectedly sweet for her. 'I was offering a reason for his being on your land. I daresay his friends were panic-stricken when they were disturbed. Was his death an accident?'

'It does not seem like it,' said Mr Brand, returning to peruse his letter once more, 'though no one has been called to account for the killing. Sir Henry says that the inquest returned a verdict that the man died at the hands of unknown persons, and there the matter rests. He says I must not trouble myself over it, but it was his duty to inform me.'

He stared at the signature on the letter. 'What manner of man can this Sir Henry be? It is all so casual. A man has died and no one seems to care.'

Abruptly he crumpled the sheet and tossed it into the empty fireplace. 'And why should I? I know nothing of the place or its people.'

Elinor watched him pace the floor a couple of times then gave a secret smile as he bent to retrieve the letter. 'It is no use, I cannot let it stand. I shall go into Gloucestershire. Oh, would that our mutual relative had willed his troublesome property elsewhere! I little knew what problems it would cause me.'

'Of which I suppose you think me one.' Elinor said sadly.

Mr Brand's shoulders lifted in a shrug. 'While I am away you and Lady Sophia can enjoy yourselves. Why should you worry?'

Why indeed? Yet Elinor knew that if her cousin was not in London to share her debut her pleasure would be spoilt. 'I would prefer it if you escorted me,' she said lamely.

'Do not fear,' Mr Brand reassured her. 'Lady Sophia will introduce you to any number of young men nearer your age and interests. You will not miss me.'

'Since you have never even questioned my interests, I fail to see how you can know what they are,' said Elinor.

'On the contrary, you made it absolutely plain to me that your chief one lies in marrying a rich husband,' he retorted coolly. 'Beside that, I imagine all others pale into nothingness.'

'Oh, you are . . . impossible,' cried Elinor. 'I cannot think why I . . .'

He raised his dark brows. 'Why you what?'

'Nothing,' she muttered.

After all the trouble she had caused she could scarcely tell him that the idea of going into society was becoming less appealing every day. She put it down to the sadness which was still so raw after her father's death. She should have waited at Miss Brown's until next year, but then she would not have become acquainted with her cousin, and she liked him. She liked him very much.

Lady Sophia, when told of Mr Brand's decision to go into Gloucestershire, accepted the news with irritation. 'You will die of boredom,' she pronounced.

Elinor's feelings could not have been so directly expressed. She was confused by her wayward thoughts. She was in London at a first-rate address, even if the house was tattered and badly kept; a lady of consequence and fashion was prepared to take her into *ton* society where she would have the entrée she needed, yet she was discontented.

Miss Tabitha's health worried her, and she spent quite a lot of time trying to induce the elderly lady to eat nourishing viands and sympathising with her as she swallowed a concoction she described as 'dreadfully bitter', prescribed by a physician. When her condition did not improve the medical gentleman recommended a stay in fresh country air, and Elinor's eyes gleamed. She wasted no time in seeing her cousin and telling him.

'It must be considered heaven-sent that you are about to take a journey into the countryside, Cousin Christopher! I have had a most capital notion. Poor Miss Tabitha shall accompany you and I will come along to care for her.'

She raised a hand as Mr Brand opened his mouth in what would clearly be a protest. 'No, I insist. I am ready to forgo my pleasure for her sake.'

She had begun lightheartedly, but a glance at her cousin's face gave her a jolt of apprehension. 'How willingly you sacrifice yourself,' he remarked.

Elinor flushed beneath his penetrating glare. 'I will tell you the truth and say that I also would be happy to spend some time in Gloucestershire.'

Mr Brand's suspicious look grew deeper and she continued, 'You have already pointed out that the Season is well advanced. Next year I shall have more time to . . .' She faltered.

'More time to find a husband,' he said.

Did she imagine the hint of scorn? She refused to be drawn into an argument with him. 'Truly, cousin, Miss Tabitha needs the country air and good farm food. She is more ill than you realise.'

Mr Brand spoke with taut patience. 'If that is indeed the case, then of course she shall be cared for. It will not be difficult to find a small cottage outside London, where you can live with Nancy to work for you. I see no reason for undertaking the expense of an expedition to the Gloucestershire estate.'

Elinor's heart thudded. 'I . . . I would like to get to know my new cousin better,' she ventured.

He gave her a long unfathomable look under which she found it almost impossible to remain still. Then he bowed. 'After such a compliment, how can I refuse?'

Elinor was wise enough to keep her peace in victory, though she had to bite her tongue when Lady Sophia, learning of the proposed journey, exclaimed, 'Well, what an amazing coincidence! My poor dear Aunt Jameson is feeling the heat quite dreadfully, and I was about to tell you that we have had an invitation to go to a friend in the country outside Bourton-on-the-Water. What great good fortune! We shall be able to visit you.'

Mrs Jameson, with her customary obedience to her niece's wishes, was doing her best to look frail as Lady Sophia continued, 'I shall be happy to give you any advice you need on the managing of so large an establishment, Miss Graham. The servants . . .'

She was interrupted by a short laugh from Mr Brand. 'They consist only of an ancient butler and his wife,' he explained. 'My lawyer tells me that the manor is barely habitable. Not really the place to which to take an ailing lady,' he ended, looking at Elinor.

Elinor pretended not to see his glance and fixed her eyes on Lady Sophia, wondering how anyone could be so blatantly obvious and so complacently brazen before she admitted privately that her ladyship's actions were no more devious than her own. She kept herself too busy planning and packing to have time to analyse her feelings, though she could not forget her awareness of her cousin's ironical looks as he listened to the two ladies agreeing with excessive politeness that next Season would be infinitely better for Elinor's prospects.

Elinor tentatively offered to help pay for the cost of transport to the country. Her cousin bowed and refused with immaculate courtesy, and informed her two days later that she and Miss Tabitha must be ready to travel at dawn the next day.

Jonas Webb had apparently been unable to dispose of a large family coach which had been cleaned and polished for their use. Harnessed to it were four horses which Elinor viewed with trepidation. 'They look sadly unmatched,' she remarked, a sentiment which was being expressed in less genteel terms by three maids, a couple of footmen and a kitchen boy from neighbouring houses.

Mr Brand's lips twisted in a grim smile. 'That is an understatement, but never fear. I shall master them.'

'You?'

'Certainly! I intend to pursue an ambition of mine, which is to tool a coach and four. Many of my friends have told me it can be an exhilarating experience.'

'Not with these nags,' declared Elinor. 'In fact, I shall be surprised if we do not end by being overset in some ditch.'

'Well, they were the best I could buy at short notice for the sum I could afford,' said Mr Brand conclusively, and Elinor was then fully occupied in allaying the fears of Miss Tabitha, who had over-heard her doubts.

Within an hour the bandboxes and portmanteaux were stowed under the seats and on the platform boot, and Elinor stepped into the carriage she was to share with Miss Tabitha, Nancy and Mr Brand's valet, a thin man in black who looked peevish.

They made reasonably good time considering the necessity to spare the horses which were to take them the entire journey and Elinor looked at the changing landscape with interest.

Beds had been bespoken at Bensington, and by the time the White Hart was reached in the late evening Elinor's enjoyment had degenerated into intense fatigue at the heat and dust, the jolting from the ill-sprung vehicle, and the frequent moans of complaint from Curtis, the valet. Miss Tabitha looked pale, but after expressing her appreciation of travelling inside instead of on the roof, she had said little, and Nancy was clearly prepared to go anywhere to escape from the hated cook at Miss Brown's school.

As Elinor prepared to step into the coach early the next day she stopped. 'Pray, Cousin Christopher, allow me to ride outside with you.' Her words had been almost involuntary, and she tried not to flinch at his raised brows. Then he shrugged. 'If you don't mind the hot sun and the dust you may.' As he picked up his gloves from the driving seat she saw that in spite of their protection his palms were blistered. She caught his hands between hers.

'Please allow me to put on some salve and bind them for you.'

He jerked his hands away. 'What nonsense! They will soon heal.'

She watched him control the horses. Even today, when they must be weary after yesterday's long haul, it was obvious that to make them pull in unison was an occupation requiring great skill and strength. She would not have supposed her cousin so capable of either, and she was able to steal more than one glance at his weary face as he wrestled with a prancing raw-boned beast which threatened continually to drag them into some ditch, while he encouraged the others to keep pace.

She was relieved when he remarked briefly that they were now climbing the lower slopes of the Cotswold Hills. Elinor looked with interest at the fields of growing crops and the fat sheep and cattle. Perhaps the lawyer had not been a good judge: if the Underhill estates presented half so prosperous an appearance there was considerable hope for the future in them. But gradually it became apparent, even to her inexperienced eye, that they were entering a part of the Gloucestershire countryside which had been disastrously neglected, and her cousin grew more grim with each mile that passed.

He halted the coach in a tiny village and asked for directions. A man dressed in a shepherd's smock, leaning on a crook, stared stonily at the enquirer. 'There b'aint no one livin' in the manor,' he stated.

'I am aware of it,' Mr Brand replied in even tones. 'I am the new owner. Will you not tell me where to go?'

'There's plenty of folk round these parts would be glad to tell the owner of the manor where to go, and it wouldn't be too polite neither.'

'Now is that the way to talk to a gentleman?' The voice came from the shadows inside a cottage door and belonged to a second man who stepped out into the evening sunlight. 'Pardon him, sir,' he begged Mr Brand, 'the crops have been poor again, and the sheep ain't doing well. Not well at all. Perhaps now we'm getting a new master things will improve.'

The words were polite, but the manner was oily. Mr Brand was curt. 'I daresay there will be time enough for me to collect opinions. Be so good as to direct me to the Underhill Manor estate.'

The man smiled, revealing a couple of broken teeth, and something in his eyes made Elinor shiver. He was as tall as her cousin; enormous muscles rippled in bare arms and his open shirt revealed thick hair as black as the mane on his head. His manner was even more unctuous as he said, 'You are already on Underhill property, sir. This is Ramscote, part of the estate, and these humble cottages belong to you. Make your bow to your master, Jed.'

Jed spat on the ground and stumped off, muttering about broken roofs and bad landlords, while the big man gave Mr Brand directions.

Her cousin whipped up the horses which began the final part of the journey and Elinor glanced back at a bend in the road to see that the man was still standing outside the cottage, arms folded, as he watched their progress from narrowed eyes.

CHAPTER
THREE

THERE could be no doubt that word had gone ahead of them, for at every cottage and farm gate folk waited to stare and Elinor felt hostility and dislike flow over them like a suffocating blanket.

They turned into a steeply rising driveway, where some long-dead owner had planted an avenue of oaks and elms which were so overgrown that they resembled a tunnel, and emerged into a park where grass grew long, before they drove past the pleasure gardens. Bindweed was strangling the shrubs and in the flowerbeds a few cultivated blooms fought vainly with dandelions. Elinor looked in dismay, but the depredations so far revealed were dwarfed by what followed.

A sharp bend in the driveway brought them within sight of Underhill Manor and Elinor gasped. Mr Brand stopped the coach and said derisively, 'Welcome to my country mansion, Elinor.'

'Well!' she exploded. 'What a farthing-pinching, miserly fellow our late relative was! Do you suppose that any money was spent on the place during his lifetime?'

'It looks as if it will be damp,' quavered Miss Tabitha from the coach window.

'And dirty,' said Elinor.

'Nothing that hard work and elbow grease won't cure,' declared Nancy.

Underhill Manor should have maintained the beautiful lines bestowed upon it by its Elizabethan builder, but ivy rioting over the walls concealed most of the warm pink bricks as well as many of the latticed windows. Slates were missing from the roof and chimneys were broken, and even the brightness of the setting sun failed to win gleams from the dirt encrusted panes.

'Did you write to say we were coming?' Elinor asked.

'Naturally I did, but clearly it needs far more than two old people to keep this place in order. Well, we had better see what else is offered.'

The studded front door was opened by a stooped figure with rheumy eyes. 'Welcome, Mr Brand, sir. I'm Tucker and this is my good wife, Martha.'

Martha gave a shaky curtsey. 'Please come in, sir and ladies. I haven't had time to prepare so many rooms. Perhaps your servants could help me.'

The party entered the Great Hall, which was high-domed and dominated by a central staircase leading to a gallery. A stone fireplace held a log which was smouldering and sending out smoke, which billowed gently into the hall.

'That chimney will need to be swept,' stated Nancy.

Elinor almost choked on smoke and slightly hysterical laughter as she gazed round at the dirt-encrusted oil paintings, the mouldering tapestries and curtains, the rusty suits of armour standing sentinel and the tracery of cobwebs high above their heads.

Mr Brand was giving the place a similar scrutiny, and their eyes met. 'Of course you and Miss Tabitha cannot remain. We must seek lodgings for you, and tomorrow you shall return to town. I shall follow as soon as possible.'

Elinor felt close to tears. No amount of dirt and difficulties could erode her desire to stay in the manor. 'It can soon be cleaned,' she said, emotion making her voice brusque. 'I am not afraid of a little work.'

Mr Brand turned a cool gaze upon her. 'A little work!' he repeated. 'You cannot be so optimistic as to believe that anything short of a miracle will render this place habitable.'

Elinor could have sworn a gleam of hope shone briefly in the ancient butler's eyes.

Mrs Tucker bustled forward. 'I'd best stop Joe from unloading, then,' she exclaimed with too much eagerness. 'Joe's my sister's grandson. I let him help. He's a bit simple, but he's strong and willing and me and Tucker can't always manage. I hope you don't mind, sir.'

'Not at all,' Mr Brand agreed politely. 'Nancy, you had better prevent Joe from removing the luggage. I will drive you to Stow-on-the-Wold.'

'No!' Elinor had not meant to sound so vehement and she was not surprised when her cousin looked astonished. She softened her tones and added, 'This is such a beautiful house! I *know* it can be made habitable. If Nancy and I remain you will be much more free to pursue . . . that other matter. And besides, you must be so weary—and so are the horses.'

Mr Brand raised his brows, then shrugged. 'As

you will. I think it will take the rest of the year to achieve anything significant here, but if it amuses you, then stay. Tomorrow I shall call on Sir Henry. And I daresay that you, Tucker, and your wife, will have something to say on the subject of the dead gipsy.'

There was a startling crash as Tucker blundered into the long fire-irons. 'I don't know anything about it, sir. Me and my wife keep ourselves to ourselves, and I don't think Sir Henry's at home. I heard tell he'd gone off on a tour . . . yes, that's it . . . a tour. You shouldn't have come all this way without asking him first . . .'

His wife grabbed his elbow. 'Stop your noise,' she ordered harshly. 'Come into the kitchen and help with the food.' She hustled him along, turning in the doorway at the back of the hall to say, 'Pay no heed to him. He's old and his wits go a-wandering.'

Mr Brand gave a few instructions to his valet who obeyed without speaking, his face set in ever increasing indignation.

He then spoke to Miss Tabitha, 'I shall escort you into the garden, ma'am. I caught sight of a charming bench near some rather overgrown roses, and the sun is pleasantly warm. As soon as rooms and meals are ready we shall call you.'

Somehow the elderly governess found her protests quite overruled and Mr Brand returned to face Elinor.

'Well,' he said with the suspicion of mockery which she was learning to dread, 'what now? Would you care to join me in a tour of my inheritance?'

She swept him a curtsey. 'Thank you for your gracious invitation.'

A short time was needed to show them that the remainder of Underhill Manor served only to emphasise the general air of neglect and decay, and Elinor and Mr Brand ended in the smaller of the two drawing-rooms. 'There is not one cosy place in the entire manor,' declared Elinor.

Mr Brand generously flicked the dust from a satin sofa with his immaculate handkerchief. 'Sit down, please, Elinor. We must talk.'

She obeyed, hands clasped on her lap.

'It is obvious,' pursued Mr Brand, 'that the sooner I investigate the matter of the dead gipsy, the better. Then we can leave and return to civilisation.'

Elinor said, 'I do so hate to be thwarted—and somehow, in spite of everything, I like this house. Take this room, for instance. A good fire will soon dry the damp, the carpet is more soiled than worn and can be cleaned. In fact the whole manor needs only womanly care to make it comfortable.

'You are forgetting the wet patches in the upper chambers which point to a leaking roof, the broken chimneys, the sorry state of the grounds. I admire your spirit, cousin, but not your practicality.'

'Would it cost much to effect the improvements?'

'I don't know. I have never been faced with such a problem.'

'Well,' Elinor said slowly, 'if you could find funds for the major repairs I shall be happy to use my money to stock the kitchen and pantry.'

'No!' He spoke vehemently. 'Not one penny of your money will I touch. It is good of you, Elinor, but your father left you all he had and it must go to your future. Do not lose sight of your purpose—a

Season and a rich husband.'

Her face flamed. 'Need you make it sound so dreadfully mercenary?'

'I beg your pardon. It is right of you to view your life realistically.'

She twisted her hands nervously. 'It seemed the only thing I could do,' she said. 'Now I have had more time to think . . .'

'Do not tell me you are weakening! Am I to understand that you have abandoned your resolve to beard the *ton* in its den?'

'No! Yes—that is to say . . .' Elinor looked up into his face. He was gazing down at her, his dark eyes quizzical, his face etched with tired lines.

'We should not be talking,' she exclaimed. 'You need rest and food.'

He made no attempt to move as she rose. 'You have not answered my question.'

His persistence angered her and she said quickly, 'No, I have not forgotten the necessity to find someone who can support me, but just at present I think I lack the heart for society. I was pushing myself on because my father . . . I thought he wanted it . . . but . . .'

There was a pause and Mr Brand said gently, 'If it will give you a soothing occupation to make the manor more habitable, I shall not argue further.'

Her joy flared out of proportion and she laughed delightedly at her cousin. 'Oh, you are a good sort of man! I cannot help but like you.'

He walked swiftly to the door and waited, obviously desiring her to pass through, and they followed Tucker who had arrived to conduct them to the dining-room.

Dinner proved that Mrs Tucker lacked culinary skill, and Elinor forced herself to eat scorched mutton and over-boiled vegetables while she resolved to give priority to seeking a cook. As she ladled portions of lumpy custard pudding from a dish held by Tucker, Mr Brand asked if Sir Henry Barnwall was expected to be away from home for long.

Tucker's hand jerked so violently that Elinor expected the custard to land in her lap, and grabbed at the dish to steady it while Mrs Tucker spoke from the sideboard. 'My husband gets confused, sir. Sir Henry is at home, he being a gentleman who don't believe in travel.'

The butler hurried away as soon as possible and Mr Brand and the ladies retired soon after. Elinor lay that night in a four-poster bed, the curtains drawn back to allow the soft June breeze to waft to her through the open window, carrying with it the perfume of night-scented stock which had won survival among the weeds. As she drifted into sleep she felt almost content.

After a breakfast of thick porridge and greasy bacon and kidneys Mr Brand went to survey the stable. He returned before Elinor had finished her coffee.

She asked, 'Have you found a saddle-horse?'

Mr Brand kept his voice even with obvious effort. 'Joe and I put the coach horses out in the paddock to rest and graze and I discovered an old nag which must serve. It is either that or . . . or a donkey cart.'

Elinor turned her head to hide a wayward smile and her cousin departed. Then she called for Nancy and together they went to inspect the kitchen.

She greeted Tucker, who was washing dishes, and looked about her. The kitchen was smaller than she had expected and contained very little furniture or cooking implements. She lifted a cauldron which the housekeeper was about to fill with some odious mixture she described as a boiled pudding.

'How heavy this pan is! Have you no others? Surely there should be some of copper. This is iron—and so old and dented!' She wandered over to the enormous range which occupied most of one wall, and stared at the spit, the iron chimney crane and the ladles and spoons which hung on hooks set in the wall.

'It is incredibly primitive! Is this where you do *all* your cooking?'

'It's enough,' the housekeeper replied sullenly. 'Me and my old man don't need lots of fancy kitchen stuff.'

'Well, it will not do for Mr Brand and his guests. Have you had much experience as a cook, Mrs Tucker?'

'She's had more than a young lady like yourself,' Tucker burst out.

Elinor looked at him steadily. 'If Mrs Tucker has been a housekeeper she need not purport to be a cook also. We need another maid—someone with culinary skill.'

'I thought you wasn't staying long, miss,' said Mrs Tucker in placating tones. 'I'll be glad to cook for you as long as you need.'

'I do not know when we shall leave,' said Elinor. She opened a rusting stove door. 'These are the baking ovens, are they not? How small for so large a dwelling! How could the bread have been baked and all the pies and tarts in years gone by?' She thought for a moment and said, 'I recall that at school I studied towards writing an essay about the days of Queen Elizabeth and discovered that they always had a separate bakehouse. Is there one here?'

'No!' declared Tucker.

'Yes!' said his wife simultaneously.

Elinor looked from one to the other and saw with alarm that the butler's face was an unpleasant purplish colour. 'Are you ill?' she asked.

'No, I'm not ill, thank you, miss,' gasped Tucker. 'I reckon I'm just too old for . . .'

'Hush now,' admonished his wife. 'It's like this, miss, there was a bakehouse, but seeing as no one used it we had it bricked up. The door used to be behind that big cupboard.'

Elinor walked to the cupboard which reached almost to the high ceiling and opened it. Inside was an assortment of unmatched dishes, cutlery and mixing bowls lying in no particular order, pieces of cheese, some of which were thick with mould, empty spice and other sundry bottles, and pots containing stale substances which Elinor preferred not to try to identify.

Mrs Tucker spoke so close to her elbow that she started. 'I know it's not orderly, but no one's cared for years.'

'Well, now someone does care. Nancy shall help you, but we must have some more women in, and men to weed the pleasure gardens and shrubbery. It must all have been so lovely once.'

'No one'll come here,' Tucker said, in a quavering voice, 'so there's no sense in your asking.'

Elinor looked at him in amazement. 'But the people on the estate are clearly in need of money.'

'No one'll come,' repeated Tucker stubbornly and Elinor began to wonder if Mrs Tucker's great-nephew, Joe, was the only simpleton around.

'By the way, where is Joe?' she asked.

Again the butler looked as if he might be about to choke. 'He . . . he's gone on an errand,' he gasped.

Elinor gazed at him in concern. 'Should you not see a physician?' she asked kindly.

'He's not ill,' declared Mrs Tucker, 'but he's getting on in years—we both are—and shocks don't come easy on us.'

'Shocks? The inspection by a gentleman of his newly acquired property? Well, the fact remains that we are here and we cannot live in the conditions prevailing. So, I repeat, where should I apply for extra servants?'

'And I tell you that they won't come,' Tucker said loudly. 'The place be . . . be haunted!'

Nancy, who had been prowling about the kitchen examining the various antiquated tools, looked up sharply. 'I don't like ghosts,' she declared. 'Have you got ghosts here?'

Mrs Tucker glared at her husband and said, 'Of course not. Leastways, I don't believe in hauntings myself, though they do say there's been some bad deeds done in the past, and it's well known that an unquiet spirit won't rest.'

'And there's some say they've heard strange noises and seen . . . mysterious appearances,' put in Tucker.

'I see,' replied Elinor. 'I shall search in the library

for the house records and try to identify your hauntings.' Her face brightened. 'I've always thought I
would like to see a ghost. Maybe I shall be lucky.'

Tucker threw her a look of near despair. 'You
want to see a ghost?'

'I think I do,' agreed Elinor.

'But ghosts be terrible things,' argued the butler.
'They . . . they rattle and groan . . . and make big
bumping noises and a kind of hammering and such
like, and . . .'

'Big bumping noises? Are you sure? I thought
they were wraithlike creatures who floated around
wringing their hands and occasionally rattling
chains.' She put a hand to her head. 'How did I
become embroiled in this ludicrous conversation? I
do not at all want to discuss ghosts, Tucker, unless
they are former cooks or gardeners. I see that I shall
have to apply to some local lady for help in the
matter of domestics.'

'No, don't do that, miss!' Mrs Tucker spoke urgently. 'I'll find someone, never fear.'

There was an almost febrile quality to her voice,
and Tucker looked ready to collapse.

Elinor turned to Nancy. 'Perhaps you could bring
down the gowns which became crumpled, and Mrs
Tucker will find you a smoothing iron.'

Mrs Tucker acknowledged the order with a curtsey and Elinor left to discover Miss Tabitha in the
garden, walking along herb-scented paths between
box hedges of rampant over-growth.

'What a beautiful place,' breathed the ex-
governess, forestalling Elinor's apology for so decrepit a dwelling. 'The only chimneys I can see are
the ones on the manor and those peeping over the

hills and treetops, and scarce one is emitting smoke. And although the gardens have been sadly neglected, they smell so fresh! I do thank you for bringing me here.'

Before such unselfish humility Elinor was silenced. She looked about her, wondering how many hours would be required to bring some order into the grounds when she caught a movement behind the high hedge which sheltered the Elizabethan garden. She darted through an arched opening and came upon a gangling youth who was peering through the straggling top leaves at Miss Tabitha. He turned in alarm and stammered incoherently while his pale blue eyes rolled in his head. Elinor withheld a rebuke as it occurred to her that this must be Joe of the weak intellect. She smiled encouragingly.

'Don't be afraid. I am not cross, though you should not spy upon us.'

Joe grinned, 'Spy? I'd make a good spy, I reckon. I make a good messenger, don't I miss? I took Aunty's message to Ramscote. I took it to Eli Bastable. Eli saw your carriage when you went through the village. He talked to you, he did. I took the message. Mrs Tucker said it was important.'

'I see. Would Eli Bastable be a big man with large muscles, long black hair and broken teeth?'

'That be him!' Joe became excited. 'He's a good fighter, miss. He could floor you with a facer if you tried to touch him.'

'I had not considered engaging in fisticuffs with Mr Bastable,' Elinor assured him. 'Did he entrust you with an answer for Mrs Tucker?'

'An answer?' Joe's mouth fell open.

'To your message, Joe.'

Joe looked terrified. 'Message? I never said nothing about a message.'

'But you cannot have forgotten! Only a moment ago, you said . . .'

'No, I never. I never took a message to nobody. Never!'

Joe turned and ran with long strides down the gravelled path and turned the corner towards the manor at high speed.

Miss Tabitha had joined Elinor and the women stared. 'What was that about?' asked Miss Tabitha.

'I wish I knew,' replied Elinor. 'The inhabitants of this place appear to have been stricken by a weird disease which turns them lunatic at frequent intervals.'

When Mr Brand returned she greeted him in the hall. He walked with the air of a man who had suffered, and said to Curtis, who materialised as his master entered the house, 'Brandy, please. I am sure you have discovered where the wines are kept.'

Curtis bowed, his lugubrious face over his black garments turning a shade more depressed. 'I have been in the cellars, sir and found a lamentably small supply of bottles containing liquid. There are many empty ones. However, fortunately it appears that those who have been drinking the cellar dry do not care for claret. There is some good claret, sir.'

'I'm surprised there is anything,' observed Elinor. 'I would have thought it had been sent for by Mr Webb.'

Curtis gave her a bow. 'From the garbled replies

of the butler I ascertained that Mr Webb did ask for the contents of the cellar, but that a good part was kept back by the servants.'

'Then bring me some, for pity's sake,' ordered his master, and he and Elinor walked to the small drawing-room where Elinor permitted her cousin to refresh himself before asking him questions.

'I saw Sir Henrý Barnwall,' explained Mr Brand. 'He is an overfed, hard-drinking, impossible man with enormous regard for himself.'

'I wonder if he found you equally attractive,' remarked Elinor demurely, as her cousin helped himself to another glass of claret.

Nancy brought coffee which Elinor poured from a pewter pot into a pink-and-gold porcelain cup. 'What an odd assortment of utensils there is here,' she remarked, but the coffee was hot and strong and she detected Nancy's hand in the making.

'The oddness extends to some of the people,' stated Mr Brand with feeling. 'Sir Henry took at least ten minutes to realise that I had not come to Gloucestershire to evaluate my new estate. He refused to believe that I was asking questions about the gipsy's death from motives other than morbid curiosity, and looked apoplectic when he learned I had left London because I was not satisfied with his brief letter.

'However, I finally got him to explain more fully. The unfortunate gipsy met his end by foul means. He had received a severe beating before being strangled with his own neckerchief.

'Then Sir Henry became agitated afresh when I told him that I was intending to make discovery of the killers my main concern.'

'What a callous man! And he is a magistrate!'

'He is far more interested in the pursuit of pleasure than performing his duties. He enjoys gossiping about the neighbourhood activities. He was interested to hear that I had ladies with me. Would you care for some diversion while you are here, Elinor?'

'I should not be human if I did not.'

Elinor expressed her gratification when informed that their arrival pleased the local gentlefolk, before she said, 'Cousin Christopher, there is a curious atmosphere about Underhill Manor.'

'I expect it is all the dust and dirt. As soon as we obtain more servants . . .'

'Must you jest? I am serious. The Tuckers veer between terror and insolence; Joe tells me he has taken messages, then denies what he has said . . .'

'Is not Joe the simple nephew of Mrs Tucker?'

'Great-nephew,' replied Elinor automatically, before she caught the implication of his words. 'You think I am being fanciful.'

'Your description, Elinor, not mine,' he pointed out.

Elinor hung on to her temper. 'I met Joe in the garden. He had been to see that big brute we met in the village. Mrs Tucker must have some connection with him.'

'My dear Elinor, Sir Henry said that all the working members of the community for miles around are related in some way. I daresay you are allowing your judgment to be swayed by the Gothic atmosphere of the manor.'

'I am not,' she replied vehemently. 'And you have just told me that Sir Henry does not want to investigate the gipsy's murder. Surely you find that indicative of mystery?'

'I find it indicative only of Sir Henry's laziness. All his ire is saved for declaiming against an outbreak of robberies which are becoming more frequent and more costly.'

Elinor found Mr Brand's grin odious as he took in her astonishment. 'Robberies? *And* ghosts?'

'Ghosts!'

'I do not believe in them,' said Elinor.

'Very wise,' approved Mr Brand. 'They have always sounded most uncomfortable to me.'

'I mean I do not believe in Tucker's ghost,' said Elinor, clutching at her shreds of forbearance.

'How can Tucker have one?' Mr Brand stretched out his booted legs. 'He is still alive.'

Elinor disregarded this flippancy. 'I am sure the Tuckers were trying to frighten me. They want us to leave the manor.'

'That is no surprise. They have had things all their own way for years. Our arrival must have been a nasty shock.'

'So you noticed it!'

'Certainly I did. Now they have to work for their keep.'

Almost through her teeth Elinor persisted, 'I know you will think it is incredible, but I begin to wonder if that old couple had a hand in killing the gipsy.'

Mr Brand sat up straight and his brows drew together. 'That will do, Elinor! Just because you are cross with me is no reason for maligning the servants. Considerable force must have been used against the dead gipsy—far more than those two possess. I am sure that Tucker and his wife simply resent being disturbed.'

'Almost as much as you resent my being here!' flashed Elinor.

Mr Brand stared at her through half-closed lids. 'You are being a foolish child,' he said. 'Perhaps you regret your impetuous decision to accompany me.'

Elinor half-opened her mouth to fling back an answer when she caught a watchful look in his eyes. 'I am glad I came,' she murmured submissively. The strain she sensed in him evaporated a little and she continued, 'The Tuckers have assumed proprietorial airs. They have bricked up the ancient bakehouse.'

'Well, it had as well remain closed, Elinor, for the more I see the less I think I shall be able to restore the manor estates to prosperity. I called on a couple of tenant farmers and was received with hostility. I cannot blame them—times are hard throughout Britain and they should have a landlord with money and knowledge of the land. What can I do? Our visit has served to convince me that if I *can* sell such a disastrous place I shall be well advised to do so.'

Elinor stared at him. 'How can you be so . . . so spineless? Who on earth will offer for a rundown heap of stones like this? Surely we can contribute something to its future prospects.'

Her flare of anger was caught by her cousin. He said softly, 'We? I must remind you that Underhill Manor is mine and my responsibility.'

Elinor's face burned. 'I apologise.' She rose. 'It seems that the Tuckers are not the only ones who regard me as an interfering interloper.'

She stalked out of the drawing-room and up to her bedchamber where she sat at the window, looking out over the Cotswold Hills, struggling with foolish tears. Why should she care about an old house and people whom she had never met? Why should it matter that a man with a modest fortune who was not even closely related should choose to keep her at a distance? She would put him out of her mind. As soon as the affair of the murdered gipsy was settled she would return to London and . . .

And what? She stirred restlessly then walked to the basin and washed her face and went downstairs, determined to ask Mrs Tucker for pails and cloths, polishes and rags, so that she and Nancy would at least bring her bedchamber to a better state. She approached the kitchen door with her graceful tread and stopped as she heard a voice which sounded faintly familiar.

'Good job you sent Joe to me,' said the voice. 'Best if I look after things from the manor.'

Elinor entered the kitchen and looked round in surprise. A number of people were seated around the large kitchen table, one of whom she recognised with a stab of apprehension.

CHAPTER
FOUR

THE man leapt to his feet and made a passable bow. Elinor said coolly, 'I saw you in Ramscote yesterday, did I not?'

'That you did, miss! Eli Bastable's the name, and I was just saying to Mrs Tucker that she did right to send for me when she saw how badly a strong pair of arms was needed.'

'Am I to understand that you have been engaged as a servant?'

'That's right, miss, and my young niece, Annie Bastable, who's a real good maid, and also this young lady here. She can do just about anything you ask, ain't that so, Betsy?'

He nudged the woman thus described and she rose, curtsied, almost fell, and sank back giggling into the chair.

Bastable bowed again. 'Me and Joe can take care of the gardening and clean the windows. In fact, this kitchen holds just about the best supply of skills in the county, ain't that so, Tucker?'

Tucker nodded his head, apparently rendered speechless by some emotion which had raised his colour again, and Elinor looked at the assembled servants. 'I shall inform Mr Brand of what has happened,' she said.

Nancy caught her arm as she emerged from the

servants' door into the Great Hall. 'Have you seen them, Miss Elinor? That great ugly man and the . . . the creature he calls Betsy? She's no better than she should be, if ever I saw one . . .'

Elinor stopped the flow of insults. 'I shall tell Mr Brand. He must decide what is to be done.'

'He's having a look at the stables, miss.'

Elinor found Mr Brand moodily regarding two thin riding mounts. 'I do not think that one single item in this whole monstrous inheritance is worth a brass farthing,' he said bitterly. 'The horse I rode this morning has a pace like a demented frog.'

Elinor refused to be drawn by the hint of abrasive humour. 'The Tuckers appear to have been engaging servants. That big man we met in Ramscote is there—Eli Bastable—and his young niece who stared at me open-mouthed. There is also a woman of low moral stature, if I am any judge.'

Mr Brand was caustic. 'And with your extensive experience of the sinful world I am sure you must be right. Well, I daresay they will do to scrub and polish for the short time we are here.'

Elinor looked at the horses. 'They require a great deal of food.'

'They require a miracle,' pronounced Mr Brand, 'as does everything attached to Underhill Manor.'

He turned and, after a moment's hesitation, proffered his arm. She stared down at the black sleeve, hesitated, then placed her fingertips upon it. They walked in silence through the kitchen garden where a small patch of vegetables had been cultivated and Elinor said, 'You mentioned robberies. Have there been many?'

'It seems so. Sir Henry said that they began about

three years ago. Little of value was stolen—mostly copper pots and other such metallic objects.'

'Copper pots! Do you suppose the ones from Underhill Manor went to the robbers?'

'Possibly! A short time ago the robberies increased in number and the goods taken were of greater value. Some families have lost their most important pieces of silver. The whole district is mystified as well as angry, for the thieves overlook jewellery, though they take money. Sir Henry himself has just lost a valuable épergne.'

Elinor frowned. 'You see, there *is* something odd about this place. And I have just thought of something exceedingly curious.'

She stopped and looked up into her cousin's face.

'That horrible man, Bastable, said that Joe had been sent to Ramscote to ask him to work at the manor, yet Joe had gone on his errand before I spoke to the Tuckers about engaging servants. Bastable hired *himself* and also his niece Annie, and the woman, Betsy.'

'What arrogance! Does it annoy you, Elinor? If so, I will send him away, and his immoral female companion. Would you wish me to dismiss the niece also?'

She felt he was teasing her, yet he sounded kind and a wave of warmth swept through her. Unexpectedly shy, she withdrew her hand as she advised, 'You had better allow them to remain, since Tucker insists that no one else will brave the Underhill ghosts.'

He laughed, then his face grew sober as he reached out and curled her fingers around his arm, patting her hand as he did so. For a moment they paced in silence, and Elinor was very conscious of their contact.

He spoke suddenly. 'Elinor, pray forgive my lack of courtesy to you earlier. The problems here do not excuse my hurting you. You are the last person I would wish to wound when I . . .'

She waited breathlessly, feeling that he had been about to say something momentous, but he paused, then asked, 'Are you positive I should not send Bastable away?'

'Not for the present, I think, though I shall look for other servants, regardless of hauntings.'

Mr Brand gave a short laugh. 'Maybe we can discover someone with a flair for valeting. Curtis has packed his belongings and departed—I am abandoned to the horrible fate of unkempt raiment and boots with only an ordinary shine.'

'Well, what a wretch the man must be!'

'I bear him no ill-will. He has stayed with me for over two years in spite of attempts to lure him from me. However, I have it on good authority that his latest tempter is a Duke, and although he has insisted always that the set of a coat on my shoulders could not be surpassed, I think the attraction of a ducal post allied to the contemplation of Underhill Manor was too much for him.'

Elinor glanced up at him from beneath her lashes. 'Can you manage without a valet? You will not think of leaving yet, will you?'

'How tenacious you are!' She held her breath, and he laughed softly and said, 'I am finding much to intrigue me here.' He slipped his arm through hers as they climbed the terrace steps into the house.

*   *   *

Luncheon proved to be excellent herb and onion omelettes, followed by a fruit pie, and Nancy explained that Annie had taken over the cooking. 'She's a nice girl, even though Eli Bastable's her uncle. He scares the wits out of her.'

Mr Brand went outside to direct operations on the garden and shrubbery and Elinor watched him from her window as he removed his coat and began to wield a billhook. He looked as if he enjoyed the rare exercise and she watched with pleasure as he swung the hook with rhythmic sweeps and cut swathes through the overgrown grass.

It was an effort to tear her gaze away, but she went to the library and, enveloped in a cotton bib-apron and mob cap of Nancy's, searched through the piles of dusty papers cluttering the drawers while Nancy climbed the library steps to begin dusting the shelves and wall panels.

Elinor closed the last bound volume of house records and sighed. The family had lived singularly uneventful lives, even managing to placate both sides in the Civil War to preserve their property and persons. There was no mention of anything which would give a reason for a ghost to prowl the manor.

The thought produced an idea and she sped to the kitchen where the new young cook gave her a startled curtsey from where she stood at the table which, Elinor noted approvingly, had recently been well scrubbed.

Annie lifted her hands, 'I'm sorry, miss, I'm all floury—can I help you?'

Elinor sniffed appreciatively. 'Where did you learn to cook?'

Annie blushed. 'My mother was cook in a gentleman's house, and she taught me. I was looking for a position and glad to come here.'

'Those omelettes were delectable. Do not disturb yourself, I wish only to speak to Tucker.'

Annie nodded towards a door. 'He's in there, but he don't want to be disturbed.'

'Indeed!' Elinor rapped smartly on the door and a drowsy voice called, 'I told you to let me be!'

'It is I, Tucker. May I enter?'

There was a hasty rustling and Tucker appeared at the door in a half-buttoned jacket, his thin grey hair awry. 'Beg pardon, miss. I couldn't know a young lady like yourself would keep coming to the kitchen.'

Elinor decided to ignore the testiness of an old man awakened from a nap and said, 'Would you be so good as to give me the butler's books? I am trying to set the housekeeping in order.'

'The . . . the butler's books?'

'Yes, and the housekeeper's books.'

Tucker seemed nailed to the spot, then his wife said from behind Elinor, 'They are over in this cupboard, miss.' She produced some large volumes. 'There's been nothing of note to write of for a long time, but I think everything's in order.'

Elinor returned to the library and began to read. It became clear that a large quantity of silver, copper and gilt utensils had vanished without record. And all the entries for some years were in the same hand.

Elinor decided to speak to her cousin and had sped halfway across the Great Hall when she realised that Mrs Tucker was showing in callers.

Her hands flew to her mob cap and she whirled

round in an effort to escape. A sight of herself in one of the long mirrors well polished by Nancy showed only too obviously how dusty and dishevelled she looked. She was about to put down her head and make a dash for the stairs when Mrs Tucker said loudly, 'Miss Graham, is that you?'

The senior lady drew back her head. 'Am I to understand that you are Mr Brand's cousin?'

Elinor made a valiant attempt at a light laugh. 'I am indeed, and I apologise for appearing before you like this, but I have been trying to bring some order to the chaos.'

The younger lady gave a simpering smile. 'Lord, Miss Graham, I would not don an apron and soil my hands for all the world.'

The male member of the trio spoke. 'How you do run on! I daresay it won't take Miss Graham a minute to arrange herself.'

The first woman said, 'I am Lady Barnwall, and this is my daughter, and my son. We were not at home when Mr Brand called and we are anxious to make your acquaintance, especially since we have had reports of you from Lady Sophia Deane.'

'Oh! Have you visited London?'

'Mamma says we have all the society we need here,' interrupted Mr Barnwall in slightly petulant accents, 'though I don't agree . . .'

Lady Barnwall waved her son to silence. 'Lady Sophia has brought her ailing aunt to stay with mutual friends. Such a sacrifice for her to make! What a good niece she is.'

Elinor was trying to come to terms with the stab of emotion she felt at this news while she asked Mrs

Tucker to show the guests into the drawing-room.

Lady Barnwall cried, 'I need no direction, Miss Graham. I once was a constant visitor here.' Her eyes devoured the grime, the cobwebs, the depredations of time and neglect and Elinor knew by her air of triumph that she would go straight to the houses of local gentlefolk to boast that she had been first to observe Underhill Manor since the arrival of its new occupants. To which she will add her impression of the appearance of Miss Elinor Graham, fumed Elinor as she sped upstairs to change.

Ten minutes later she was able to sit in the small drawing-room and observe that although the visitors were garbed in high fashion everything was too colourful or over-bedecked, and that they wore a vulgar number of jewels, fobs and watches. This gave her a certain satisfaction and when Mr Brand, having been warned, arrived in cream pantaloons and a coat fashioned by a master tailor, she had the added happiness of seeing Mr Barnwall looking extremely envious and Miss Barnwall making girlish overtures to her cousin, who responded with casual courtesy.

Mr Brand was plied with questions about London as Elinor poured coffee and Nancy handed round lemon cakes hot from the oven. Mr Barnwall attempted to open a silver-encrusted snuff-box with one fashionable fingernail, failed, and spilt snuff, causing his sister to sneeze until Elinor felt so sorry for her that she offered to lend her a clean handkerchief.

Miss Tabitha hurried in and Lady Barnwall surveyed her through an eyeglass as Mr Brand made an introduction and Lady Barnwall said graciously, 'You are a retired governess! How interesting.'

'How useful to have a governess actually in the family,' cried Miss Barnwall. 'Have we such a person among our connections, Mamma?'

'Good gracious, no!' Lady Barnwall might have been repudiating a scavenger on their family tree. 'Of course, there is nothing wrong with being a governess—a most ladylike profession, I am sure.'

Elinor's eyes sparkled with anger and Mr Brand rose hastily to his feet. He carried Miss Tabitha a cup of coffee and handed it to her with a courtly bow. 'We consider ourselves blessed to have so charming a lady upon whom to call for advice.'

A grateful smile wreathed Miss Tabitha's face and Lady Barnwall rose and announced that they must go on to other calls.

'Do you suppose they are a fair sample of the local community?' asked Elinor, when they had taken their departure.

Mr Brand gave her a sardonic glance. 'If you find Lady Barnwall and her unprepossessing offspring difficult to manage, I think you had best think twice before you enter the London *haute monde*, where you will soon discover dames far more intimidating.'

'I will face that problem if—when it arrives,' said Elinor firmly.

'Not having second thoughts, are you?'

'You seem determined to put me off the idea—for what reason, I cannot conceive.'

'Cannot you?' His voice was suddenly harsh and Elinor was startled. Then he smiled. 'A dove to the lions,' he mused. 'I can only hope that Lady Sophia decides to guard you well, Elinor.'

A dozen retorts tumbled into Elinor's brain, chief among them being a desire to tell Mr Brand exactly what she thought of her ladyship. She realised that her cousin was watching her with some amusement and had the feeling that he knew precisely what was causing her to frown. He disarmed her by holding out his arm.

'Will you walk with me in the garden?'

The roses were almost cleared of weeds and Elinor picked one, savouring the delicious summery scent.

'Do you know that your complexion is lovelier and creamier than the rose you hold?' asked Mr Brand in a voice of melting gentleness.

She felt her legs tremble beneath her and jerked the rose from her face.

'Do you not care to be complimented?'

'Only when the person means it, sir.'

'I meant it, Elinor.' His eyes were alive with sincerity.

'Papa was wont to praise my looks, but I know I am no beauty. Unlike Lady Sophia,' she concluded, then wished the words unsaid as the pleasure faded from his face.

He might have spoken further if his attention had not been drawn to someone behind her. She turned to see Eli Bastable working a few yards away. 'I do not like that man,' she protested in an undertone, yet feeling thankful that the servant had prevented what had threatened to become another reprimand from her cousin.

Mr Brand shrugged. 'He is strong and appears

willing. And his niece can cook.'

'Nevertheless I should like your permission to try to replace him.'

'You have it.' His voice was terse, and the warmth of the day was spoilt for her.

'I have been looking through the house records and find that many items of metal are missing—some of them quite valuable silver,' she said.

'Indeed! I would be more astonished to find them after Uncle Jonas had taken his pick. Take my word for it, they have gone to pay gaming debts.'

'Copper pots and pans?' she queried allowing a tinge of sarcasm to colour her voice. 'There should be six copper warming-pans as well as the four brass ones. And everything in the kitchen is made of iron. The cutlery is practically non-existent.'

'Elinor, I really do not wish to give my attention to the loss of a few pots and pans. I have more to think about.'

'I suppose those matters are woman's work,' she flashed.

'I am delighted to see that you have your priorities right.'

His grin was infuriating, and he announced that he was about to change back to his working clothes and continue his labours in the garden. She walked to the house with him in silence and ignored the amusement which lurked in his eyes.

Mrs Robinson, the wife of the rector of Ramscote Church, was a plump, smiling woman with a pleasant face beneath a starched cap. She welcomed Elinor warmly and the two ladies drank tea. The cool of the drawing-room was welcome after the heat of the walk and Mrs Robinson seemed unembarrassed by the clutter of newspapers, books and toys. She lifted a hobby-horse from the sofa, allowing Elinor to be seated.

'Of course we have heard of your arrival at Underhill, Miss Graham,' she said, sinking into an easy chair and fanning herself with a child's primer. 'I have made the acquaintance of a friend of yours— a Lady Sophia Deane, who was full of praise for the way in which Mr Brand is assuming his duties. How kind she must be to leave her many commitments in London to care for her poor aunt.'

Elinor murmured something which would pass for agreement even as she fulminated against a woman who was clever enough to pursue her goal so determinedly and at the same time make herself appear an uncomplaining martyr.

When asked to recommend servants, Mrs Robinson shook her head regretfully. 'I agree that there is much poverty here, but I fear that you will have no success in engaging different servants. I know Bastable is a rogue, and Betsy . . .' Her voice trailed off and a slight flush mantled her homely features.

'I hate to think I must keep them,' protested Elinor.

'I should feel the same, my dear. I still have five children at home and would not for a moment countenance . . . still, you are all adult at the manor.'

She fanned her face vigorously then said abruptly, 'Fearful tales have been circulating regarding Underhill—there has been much talk of ghosts and strange occurrences. My husband, the Rector, insists that it is all moonshine, but since the awful killing of the young gipsy . . .'

'Tucker has already mentioned the hauntings,' said Elinor. She felt gloomy at the idea that she would have to endure the presence of two servants who engendered unease and even disgust in her.

Mrs Robinson spoke again. 'Pray, do not be despondent, Miss Graham. I daresay it is all exaggerated. Let us discuss something more pleasant. I am giving a garden luncheon party three days from now. Just music, pleasant company, food—we would welcome you and your companions.'

Elinor was delighted to accept and she and Nancy strolled home between high hedges where birds chirrupped, through byways knee-deep in moon-daisies and buttercups which dusted their shoes with pollen. Her senses were almost drugged by the hot scents of summer, and by the time they reached the wicket gate into the grounds of the manor she had begun to persuade herself that she must be imagining the strange atmosphere.

She and Nancy entered the belt of trees spanning the estate and walked beneath an ancient sycamore. The sudden transition from bright sunlight to deep shade blinded her for a few seconds, so that it seemed as if the figure which appeared must have been spirited there.

The girl was a gipsy of about her own age. Thick jet hair flowed over her shoulders in an inky stream, her black eyes were mesmeric in their stare and her cheeks a deeper pink than the dog-roses in the hedgerows. Her sensual scarlet mouth curved in an ingratiating smile and she lowered her eyes to a wicker basket and said in a professional whine,

'Buy some wild herbs, lady? I've campion for the stomach or ragwort for the throat. Any pots and pans to mend, lady?'

Elinor gently detached Nancy's fingers, which had clutched her arm convulsively. 'Are you on your way to the manor?' she asked.

The girl's face twisted in a spasm which could have been fear or hate. 'The manor! That's where we be going.'

'We?'

The girl spoke softly and a tousle-haired urchin with bare feet scurried from a thicket and stood half-hidden by her skirts. 'This be Jacky, my young brother. Our ma and pa be dead and I look after him and four others.'

Nancy urged Elinor in a whisper to leave. The gipsy's ears were as sharp as those of the wild animals whose existence she shared. 'Not frightened, be you? I wouldn't hurt you.'

'I do not suppose you would,' replied Elinor coolly. Then, thinking of that odd expression, she asked quickly, 'Has anyone from the manor harmed you?'

For a moment there was silence, but to Elinor's taut nerves it seemed as if the dancing leaf-shadows took on a quality of smoke as the girl's eyes blazed and her red mouth twisted. She smiled. 'Harmed me!' She put her hand into the basket. 'Buy some of my herbs, lady? I got good ones for the cooking pot.'

This was too much for Nancy who cried, 'My mistress isn't interested in cooking, and most likely you stole these plants from Underhill estate. Be off, insolent woman!'

The gipsy girl tossed her head. 'Be careful how you talk to Zenobia. I come from an old royal line, and I've got secrets you never dream on.'

Nancy had begun to tremble and Elinor said, 'You should not frighten my maid. If you wish to proceed to the kitchen, please do.'

She hurried away, hearing the soft laugh given by Zenobia and sensing the fiery eyes on her back.

Nancy dared a glance back. 'She's just standing staring after us.'

Elinor found her cousin in the library and told him of her encounter. 'There was something almost—diabolical about that girl,' she ended.

Mr Brand gave her a derisive grin. 'More mystery!' He looked deliberately about at the half-empty shelves. 'I regret there are no novels at all, Elinor. Let me guess at your favourite type of reading. How about *The Mysteries of Udolpho*, or perhaps *The Monk*—which I believe is excessively full of horror?'

Elinor breathed hard. If she had not been gently bred she felt she might have picked up one of the largest books and thrown it into his tantalising face. His grin deepened. 'Don't try, my dear.'

'You are impossible!' she declared. 'You believe in nothing which you cannot actually see.'

He shrugged and spread his hands. 'Elinor, you are hot and agitated and your nerves have been cruelly stretched over the past months. You must allow yourself to relax. Make the most of your stay in the country and forget all these odd fancies.'

At the beginning of his speech she had warmed to his concern, but now she flushed angrily. 'I have not any odd fancies,' she stormed. 'I feel that something here is not as it should be.'

'I would be the last man in the world to disagree with you there.'

'You misunderstand me deliberately!'

'Temper!' he chided mockingly, and she turned and walked swiftly to the door. 'Bring me a shred of proof that the enigmas do not spring from your imagination and I will believe,' he called after her, and she had to restrain an impulse to slam the heavy library door behind her.

CHAPTER
FIVE

SHE went to the kitchen to see if Annie was coping adequately and as she walked down the corridor she heard a muffled scream, then a plea for mercy and ran the last few steps and opened the door. Eli Bastable whirled round and released the woman who struggled with him. Betsy had a rapidly purpling bruise on her cheek and her hair was even more untidy than usual. She rubbed one of her arms.

Bastable grimaced. 'I was chastising the wench. She's supposed to be working and I found her asleep.'

'You should not strike her!'

'I didn't hit her hard. She knows no other punishment, do you, Betsy? You don't hold it against me, do you?'

The maid shook her head sullenly.

'Nevertheless, Bastable, you will not strike a maid beneath this roof or Mr Brand will dismiss you. Is that understood?'

'Perfectly, Miss Graham,' he answered in unctuous tones. 'I'll have to think of other ways to punish you, won't I, Betsy!'

He leered and Elinor said sharply, 'The maids are Mrs Tucker's concern. Why are you not outside?'

'Poor Tucker asked me to help him. He's such a weak old man and Mrs Tucker can't control this she-cat. But I'll go straight back into the garden,

miss. Mr Brand asked for vegetables to be planted.
Does that mean you're staying on for winter, miss?'

Annie, who had been standing by the range looking terrified, gasped at his insolence and Elinor
raised her brows. He touched his forehead. 'Beggin' your pardon, miss, I just wanted to make sure
that there'll be enough logs cut.'

'Address your questions to Mr Brand,' ordered
Elinor. She hurried back to the library. She had
meant to tell Mr Brand at once of Bastable's disgraceful behaviour, but found instead that she
could not wait to put the question Bastable had
raised. She wondered why the answer suddenly
meant so much to her as she asked, 'Shall we be
in Underhill Manor for the winter, Cousin Christopher?'

He looked up from a letter he was writing and the
expressive brows rose. 'Back so soon? I thought
you did not relish my company.'

'Bastable wants to know,' she replied distantly.

'Does he, indeed?'

'He has apparently taken over the running of the
manor.'

'Well, someone should. It was in a sorry state in
the Tuckers' care.'

'I collect you do not object to such a villain managing your affairs?'

'Villains, my dear Elinor, manage a great
number of affairs in many walks of life.'

She stared at him and his dark eyes mocked her.
She had a sudden urge to plead for an answer. She
could not—would not analyse her reason for finding his decision so vital. The mockery died from his
face and he half-rose in his chair, then sank back.

'I think we may be here for longer than I antici-pated. I shall let you know later.'

'Is that all you can say?' Her tension was released in an explosion of fury. 'Do you take a perverse delight in keeping me upon a string like some puppet?'

'Is that how you see yourself?' His tone was genuinely curious. 'It would seem to me that lately you have been responsible for directing your life without advice from anyone.'

'I am only attempting to do what I feel is right for me.'

'And why not?' Again the tinge of mockery showed. 'Well, my dear Elinor, I have given the only answer I can. Later I may have it in my power to tell you more. As for Bastable, he can go to hell.'

'Do you expect me to tell him that? I just caught him striking Betsy!'

He was as lithe as a cat in his movement as he left his chair and reached her side. She scarcely dared meet his gaze as he asked harshly, 'He did not threaten you, did he? If I thought . . .'

'He has made no physical threat,' she said quickly, 'but his manner is so . . . so impossibly rude!'

She was finding articulation difficult as her cousin stood over her. Again she knew an impulse to touch him—to caress away the angry lines from his thin face. The idea so startled her that she took a step back.

'Frightened of me also? You need not be, I do assure you.'

'Of course I am not! You are my . . . my cousin and my . . . my friend.'

A one-sided smile twisted his mouth. 'Why, so I am, my dear.' He re-seated himself and picked up his pen. 'Pray excuse me, Elinor. I have an important letter to finish.'

Thus dismissed she walked away feeling a sense of loss. At the door she turned. 'We have been invited to the parsonage for a garden lunch. Will you take us?'

'If it will amuse you,' he replied, not looking up from his writing, and with that she had to be content.

It took courage to enter the library again a few moments later and she was not surprised when Mr Brand gave her an exasperated look. 'What now, Elinor?'

'I have thought of something else.'

'Pray go on!'

'The kitchen was extremely hot.'

'I daresay that was because it is June and the temperature high.'

She forced herself to maintain control. 'The fire was low and the windows and door open, yet the heat was intense. And Betsy's face was red and perspiring.'

'So would mine if Bastable were attacking me.'

'Can you never be serious?'

'Often,' he replied. 'For instance, I am very serious about this letter. I wish it to go as soon as possible.'

This time she did bang the library door, though it was too heavy to make a satisfactory crash, and went upstairs to look out a gown for the parsonage party.

*　　　*　　　*

At dinner that night Elinor maintained an air of remoteness towards her cousin, who seemed to find it diverting. He persisted in addressing her on subjects ranging from the poor condition of his newly-acquired land to the fashion in bonnets prevailing that year. Elinor answered everything with studied calm and she was consequently furious with herself for showing immediate interest when Mr Brand said casually, 'I went to find the gipsy camp today.'

Miss Tabitha looked at him with scared eyes, 'How brave of you! I would not dare.'

Elinor exclaimed unthinkingly, 'You might have taken me with you!'

Mr Brand smiled. 'I decided you had had enough excitement for one day.'

She could not resist plying him with questions. 'What were they like? Did you see Zenobia? Did you gain an idea of why she looked so strangely at me?'

'The answer to all your queries is no,' he replied, becoming intent on peeling a peach. 'How juicy this is,' he remarked. 'Did you know that Lady Barnwall sent us a basket of fruit Elinor? It came with a note saying she knew that the trees in Underhill have grown stunted and barren. Was not that kind of her?'

'Immensely,' said Elinor. 'What happened when you reached the camp?'

'Nothing, because I did not reach it.'

'But you said . . .'

'I said I went to find it. I did not tell you I succeeded.'

'Oh, you allowed me to believe . . .'

Miss Tabitha was shocked into speech. 'Elinor,

you should not address a gentleman in such angry tones, my dear. It is unbecoming.'

'That is perfectly true,' agreed Mr Brand, laying the last piece of peach-skin on the side of his plate and dipping his long fingers into a finger-bowl. 'What a blessing that these are made of plain glass, or presumably they would have gone the way of all the other precious objects here.'

Elinor would have found great satisfaction in tipping the contents of the bowl over her cousin's head. She was searching for something scathing to say when unexpectedly he offered her the plate on which lay the peach, its soft flesh oozing pearls of moisture.

She took the plate and her eyes met her cousin's. Something flickered in their dark depths and her desire to anger him fled. She cut a slice of the fruit with a small knife and put it into her mouth. The juice caressed her tongue with sweetness and she swallowed the mouthful before asking, 'Did you find no trace of the encampment?'

'I went to a place described to me by a local farmer. The ground was still hot from cooking fires, but there was no sign of the gipsies. Perhaps they have moved on.'

Elinor recalled the expression on Zenobia's face and a slight shiver ran through her. She did not think they had seen the last of the gipsy tribe, but she kept her opinion to herself. Somehow the atmosphere between herself and her cousin had become as soft and mellow as the peach she ate, and she did not wish to spoil it.

The weather for the parsonage party was as fine and

warm as any during this hot summer. Mr Brand appeared in strapped pantaloons, a morning coat and a tall hat, and announced that a passable landau had been discovered in the carriage house and been cleaned and polished by Joe. Two horses which had benefited from even a few days of good living had been curry-combed and brushed, and after Miss Tabitha had been assisted into the body of the carriage Elinor, feeling unreasonably elated, sat beside her cousin as he took the reins.

It was evident that the living was a good one. Expense had not been considered and the parsonage lawns were shady with awnings, while maids in impeccable garb plied the guests with a quantity of excellent food and drink.

Mr Brand was quickly appropriated by gentlemen anxious to discuss his inherited land and offer advice, Miss Tabitha was pleased to seat herself among the dowagers, and Elinor was introduced to several young men, among them Mr Robinson's curate.

'I can leave you safely with Mr Hawkins,' said Mrs Robinson with a slightly arch smile, 'and later you will have the pleasure of meeting your friends, Lady Sophia and her aunt. They have promised to attend my little party.'

Involuntarily Elinor's eyes flew to the group which held her cousin. Her ladyship was clearly determined not to let him slip away from her.

Mr Hawkins bent over her and asked, 'Are you unwell, Miss Graham? You look rather—disturbed.'

'Unwell? Certainly not, sir. I have never felt better.' He smiled and escorted her around the gardens where many couples strolled and chattered. She found it difficult to concentrate on anything he said, for her attention was directed to the arched rose trellis through which all guests must pass to join the party. It was not long before Lady Sophia's clear tones reached her.

'London is so enervating and my poor aunt could not bear it. So I have brought her into the country. Yes, dear Mrs Robinson, it did mean that I was forced to cancel several quite attractive engagements, but when duty calls me I am never slow to respond.'

She greeted Elinor's appearance with exaggerated delight. 'I was so hoping to find you here, Miss Graham. Do you know the Polite World is astonished that Mr Brand left London before the end of the Season?'

'I am sure you were able to enlighten the enquirers as to his reasons,' replied Elinor, as she rose from her curtsey.

'I did indeed. And they were amazed at his self-sacrifice.' She looked over Elinor's shoulder. 'Dear Mr Brand, we meet again.' He bowed over her hand and she murmured, 'London was not the same without you, sir.'

'How charming of you to say so, Lady Sophia. How are you, Mrs Jameson? Recovering well in the country air, I hope.'

Mrs Jameson managed to appear a little frail by leaning on the arm hastily extended by Lady Sophia. 'Yes, thank you, sir. I feel much improved.'

'Perhaps you will assist me in escorting my aunt to a shady place, and then walk with me in the flower gardens,' Lady Sophia suggested.

Elinor was shaken by her direct approach, but Mr Brand only laughed. 'I shall be happy to do so.'

He and Lady Sophia settled Mrs Jameson comfortably and were about to leave her when a commotion near the trellis turned all heads.

A stout country squire, his lady and their offspring were making a loud clamour as they attempted to talk all at once. Elinor caught the word 'robbery' before she and the curate hurried to the table where Mr Robinson was directing servants to serve the agitated family with refreshments.

The squire mopped his brow. 'Last night those villains broke into my house for the second time. It was bad enough when they removed the copperware and stole many guineas, but now they have purloined the silver.'

His wife dabbed her eyes. 'Mamma's elegant candle-holders which she left me, the inkstand once owned by my dear husband's grandpapa, our best dishes—all gone!'

Lady Barnwall pushed herself forward. 'I have said many times that I believe this to be the work of the gipsies. Whenever they make camp here the robberies increase.'

Mr Brand protested, 'Surely if they behaved in so stupid a manner they would know they were the chief suspects. Perhaps someone is using their presence as a cover.'

Elinor approved this reasoned argument, but voices on all sides were raised against it. 'It is easy for you to talk,' said a man in an embroidered waistcoat. 'We all know that Jonas Webb left nothing worth the taking.'

'It is not to be borne,' a gentleman farmer shouted. 'Who is with me in a search for the miscreants?'

They were galvanised into activity and Mr Brand had no choice but to accompany them on the hunt leaving the bereft females to enjoy the party as best they might. They returned in something over an hour to report that all known camping spots were empty, but that the search would continue. They then escorted the women home and embarked on a more thorough investigation.

It was dark when Mr Brand entered the manor where he accepted a glass of claret poured for him by Elinor. 'What an expedition! We finally tracked the gipsies to a spinney on Mr Robinson's land. No one had thought of looking so close to the village, but one of Sir Henry's dogs sniffed them out.'

'Dog? That's barbaric!'

Mr Brand made an impatient gesture. 'You are being over-dramatic. The dogs did not harm them, and if the gipsies are guilty of thieving they should be apprehended.'

'You said "if". Has any proof been found?'

Mr Brand leaned back in his chair and stretched out his legs, groaning a little. 'The area around the camp was searched, but nothing was discovered. The gamekeepers are sure that the ground offered no evidence of anything being buried, but . . .' He shrugged. 'There are a hundred places where stolen goods could be concealed.'

He took another drink of wine and stared ahead, his face grim. 'Sir Henry and some of the other men decided that the gipsies must move anyway. Mr Robinson refused. There is a woman about to bear a child, and the birth is imminent.'

'Did not Sir Henry feel any compassion?'

'He seems not to regard travelling folk as human, but the Rector insisted that the gipsies were on his land and would be allowed to remain, so they are still in Ramscote.' He finished his wine. 'I suppose Miss Tabitha is in bed. It is fortunate that the summer light allowed us to complete our search.'

'Do *you* think the gipsies are innocent?'

'Who knows? Is there something to eat? I am famished.'

Elinor was contrite, and tugged the bellpull by the fireplace. When no one answered she frowned. 'Now what? No, do not disturb yourself. I will go to the kitchen.'

She took a candle-holder and walked along the corridor leading to the servants' quarters. It was unlit and she moved cautiously for the tiny gleam did little to relieve the blackness and brought no illumination at all to a pile of pans which clattered loudly as she bumped into them.

From inside the kitchen there were sounds of hasty movement, a scraping noise and a muffled oath, but when she entered she saw only Annie, who clung to the mantelshelf and gazed at her with wide, terrified eyes.

'Where is Nancy?' asked Elinor. 'Why were those pots left out in the dark? Why did you not answer the bell?'

'N . . . Nancy is with Miss Claypole, who has a headache,' said Annie in a hoarse whisper. 'I'm sorry about the pots. I . . . I forgot to move them.'

Annie's upper lip was damp and Elinor was sorry for her burst of temper. 'You look ready to faint,

Annie. What has upset you? You had better sit down.'

'I must help you, miss,' Annie protested, but her trembling legs forced her to subside in a chair.

She was clearly useless and Elinor asked, 'Where are the Tuckers? Mr Brand needs food.'

'Gone to bed. They're old, and they get tired easy.'

That at least sounded reasonable and Elinor decided to fend for herself. She looked into the large cupboard which contained the same unsavoury mess. 'Where is the food kept?' she demanded, trying to keep exasperation from her voice.

Annie gestured to a door which led to a pantry where Elinor loaded a tray, trying as she did so to calm the maid. 'We are both delighted with your cooking. Mr Brand will enjoy this piece of beefsteak pie and some lemon cheesecakes.'

'Yes, miss. Thank you, miss.' Annie's voice held no gratification, and Elinor gave up. 'Will you bring a tray of tea to the small drawing-room, Annie?'

Her cousin leapt to his feet when he saw her with the loaded tray. 'What is this? Are you a servant?'

Elinor smiled. 'Tonight I serve you, cousin. Pray, sit down and do not fuss.'

As Mr Brand ate she told him of the odd atmosphere in the kitchen. He seemed unimpressed. 'You are still remembering Tucker's ghosts,' he mumbled through a piece of pie. 'Mmmm, this is delicious.'

Elinor felt the familiar flash of anger at his dismissal of her suspicions, but held her tongue. He looked very weary.

She checked that Miss Tabitha had a soothing

draught for her headache and went to bed. Perhaps
the alarms of the day caused the disjointed dreams
and when she awoke suddenly she thought she was
still dreaming. But the sounds continued after she
was fully awake. She felt a shiver of fear run up her
back. Exactly as Tucker had described, there were
banging and clanging noises. They echoed weirdly
through her room and when the hammering stopped a murmur of disembodied voices susurrated
round the walls.

Elinor's skin prickled and she began to shake. To
joke about supernatural manifestations in daylight
was one thing; to experience them alone in the dead
of night, another entirely!

The banging started once more and she lit her
candle. The room was empty and she forced her
trembling legs out of bed, pushed her feet into her
pumps and dragged her shawl about her shoulders.
She made her movements deliberate in an effort to
convince herself that she was not afraid.

The noises sounded stronger on one side of the
room and she padded across and laid her ear to the
wall. Someone—something?—was causing inex-
plicable sounds inside her wall. All reason deserted
her and she fled in a panic from her bedchamber to
her cousin's room, where she beat her fists on the
door panels.

Mr Brand's voice came sleepily. 'Who is it?'

'Cousin Christopher, can I come in?' Elinor
called.

'Good God! Elinor? What on earth . . .?'

There was a rustling sound, quick footsteps and
Mr Brand appeared holding a candle with one hand
and clutching his dressing-gown about him with the

other. 'What in heaven's name ails you? Are you ill?'

'No, not ill. I very much fear your house is haunted—j . . . just as Tucker said. Did you hear them?'

'Them?'

'The banging and clattering—the voices?'

At his astounded look Elinor knew that he had heard nothing. 'Listen,' she begged.

They heard only the screech of an owl as it went about its gory business of night feeding, and the lowing of a cow.

'They *were* there,' insisted Elinor. 'Weird, strange noises!'

Mr Brand concealed a yawn behind his hand. 'Oh, Elinor, I daresay you were dreaming. Perhaps you should not have eaten those cheesecakes.' He placed the candle-holder on a side table and tied his dressing gown cord.

'Are you implying I have *indigestion?*'

He was apologetic. 'It can cause quite nasty sensations.'

She almost stamped her foot. 'I did hear the noises—I did! I did! Whenever I try to tell you anything about this place, you turn the talk into something idiotic.'

He had been smiling, but slowly his expression altered and his lids narrowed. Abruptly Elinor realised that her shawl was gone and she stood only in her nightgown. Its fine lawn was no less modest than a muslin gown, but in an instinctive movement she crossed her hands beneath her chin, covering her breasts with her arms. Her eyes widened as her cousin took a step nearer. 'Elinor . . .' he breathed.

She knew she should run from him, but some undefined emotion was taking her over. She moved her feet, but not away from him. A step brought her so close that she could feel the warmth of his body through the thin cotton of her gown.

'Elinor . . .' he said again, as his hands reached out and gripped her arms above the elbows.

She turned her face up to his and stared into the depths of his eyes.

She had never known desire, but she recognised it now. Slowly, hypnotically, his head came down and warm, searching lips were on hers. Every instinct within her ached to respond. Her lips parted and as his hands moved to her waist her own began to steal around his neck.

Then, with an abruptness which gave her actual physical pain, he thrust her from him and looked over her shoulder.

Elinor whirled round to see Bastable, fully dressed, staring at them with a slight grin. He touched his forehead, 'Beg pardon, sir and miss. I didn't mean to stop you . . . er . . . I was checking all the doors and windows—you can't be too careful with robbers about. I thought I heard a woman cry out and came to see if everything was all right.'

His words and looks conveyed an insolence which was yet subtle enough to defy reprimand. Elinor licked her lips. 'I . . . I cried out, Bastable. Did you hear the . . . the strange sounds?'

'Strange sounds, miss? I only heard the cry. Was it you, miss? I'm sorry, sir, I wouldn't have come up if I'd know you was . . . looking after Miss Graham.'

Mr Brand's voice was not quite controlled as he

replied, 'You are right to make sure the manor is secure, though there is nothing in it to interest robbers.'

'What is the time?' asked Elinor.

'Half past one o'clock,' said Bastable.

'You keep late hours,' she said. She should have remained silent and not given him another opportunity to speak. Her mortification was complete when she realised that he was holding her shawl. 'You dropped this, I expect.'

Elinor dared not stir. She was standing in shadow beside the candle, but to move would throw her body into relief against its light. Her cousin stepped forward and shielded her as he took the shawl.

'Thank you, Bastable. That will be all.'

'Thank *you* sir. I'll be off to my bed, then.'

Elinor grabbed her shawl and wrapped it about herself as they watched the big man walk away. 'He must have eyes like a cat,' said Elinor. 'Or perhaps he prefers to spy on us in the dark.'

She was in an agony of embarrassment as she waited to see what her cousin would do and say, and she was oddly disappointed when he remained two paces from her and asked if she would like him to come to her room to listen for the sounds. Perhaps it was only her overwrought imagination which made her think that he was simply humouring her.

'I did hear them,' she said weakly.

Without answering he strode along the corridor and she hurried after him. By now it was no surprise to find that there was not a hint of noise anywhere in her bedchamber.

Mr Brand bowed and placed his candle on her

bedside table. 'I daresay you were dreaming, Elinor. Sleep well.'

The door clicked behind him and she climbed into bed, weary beyond understanding, and she lay until the first birds sang, thinking about her cousin, wondering how she would face him in daylight.

Her cheeks burned. He knew nothing of her except what she had told him. He might begin to wonder if she made a habit of enticing men. She almost squirmed in her humiliation. And not the least of her worries was the realisation that overlying everything was her intense pleasure at the memory of his lips on hers, his hands about her body.

She finally slept and awoke to a day of summer brightness which mocked her fear. Only her cousin appeared at the breakfast table, and he remained coolly polite until in perverse exasperation she said, 'I beg your pardon for disturbing you in the night.'

She immediately wished she had held her peace as he looked at her steadily. 'It is right that you should call on me if you are worried. As for disturbing me . . .' He took a sip of hot coffee and stared at her over the rim of the cup before placing it deliberately back in the saucer. She waited for him to finish his sentence, but he rose suddenly.

'I had better begin work outside before the heat of the day becomes uncomfortable.' He left his coffee unfinished and Elinor lost her appetite and wandered to the window.

Through it she saw her cousin striding towards the garden. Joe followed him with a wheelbarrow of tools. If Mr Brand were not so evidently a gentleman, one might have mistaken him for a gardener.

He wore leather breeches, a frilled shirt with sleeves rolled up over surprisingly muscular arms, and a loosely-tied brown spotted cravat. His hair was ruffled by the soft breezes which carried the scent of turned earth and plants through the open lattice, and the mingled perfumes and her capricious feelings brought her close to tears.

She swallowed them as Bastable appeared in the garden, at his heels a savage-looking lurcher dog. The man had the instincts of an animal and turned sharply as he felt her eyes upon him. He bowed and touched his forelock unctuously, at the same time smiling in a knowing way which made her burn, as he walked to the window. 'I hope you're all right after last night, miss.'

She managed to keep her voice level. 'I am, thank you. I do not recall seeing your dog before.'

'No, miss. I've kept him at home until now, but I thought he'd be useful with all the night prowlers about, miss.'

She stared into his sneering face. 'Do not let me detain you. You have work to do.'

'That I have, miss. I'll go and help Mr Brand, then. He's much stronger than I thought a London gentleman would be. Got a lot of strength to him, hasn't he, miss?'

Elinor turned away and pretended not to hear the servant's laugh.

CHAPTER
SIX

ELINOR went to see why Miss Tabitha was still in bed, and found the small ex-governess very apologetic. 'I cannot think why I should have such a headache,' she said. 'I will rise soon.'

'You will stay there until you are completely well,' Elinor ordered gently, and kissed the pallid face impulsively.

As she left to go downstairs she thought soberly that the fate of women without fortune was hard indeed. What else was there to do but seek out and manage to marry a rich husband? She was shaken suddenly when the memory of her cousin's lips came to torment her, and she shook herself angrily. What right had he to touch her? He had never felt the need to marry, and if he changed his mind now because of poor people who needed him he would choose a woman of substance. Someone like Lady Sophia!

Later she was directing Nancy and Mrs Tucker as they tackled the cleaning of the hall, and wielding a duster herself, when a carriage was heard on the sweep of the gravel drive.

'Not more visitors,' she groaned. 'Why will they not give us time to settle?' She managed to tear off her apron as Nancy opened the door and took the silk shawls and parasols of Lady Sophia and Mrs Jameson.

Lady Sophia looked around her with an amused laugh. 'I heard that you were having a difficult task in putting the manor to rights, Miss Graham, but I did not really believe you were actually undertaking menial tasks yourself.'

Her eyes strayed to Elinor's head, reminding her that she had forgotton to remove her mob cap. She snatched it off with what she hoped was a humorous laugh. 'There is much to do and few to do it,' she said. 'I am quite enjoying the work.'

'Really!' Lady Sophia strolled to the centre of the Great Hall. 'What an odd sentiment—I think you are teasing me. I would not know how to tackle house-cleaning if my life depended on it.'

Elinor stifled the unworthy wish that her ladyship's life did depend on so slender a thread as Lady Sophia said, 'What a handsome residence this must once have been. And could be again if money were spent.' She gingerly touched a rusty suit of armour. 'Mr Brand is not a wealthy man.'

'I am not familiar with my cousin's means of support,' flashed Elinor.

'Are you not? Well, I can tell you that what he requires is the help of someone with funds.'

Elinor's fulminating response was not uttered as Mr Brand entered the hall. 'Pray, excuse my appearing in such rough and dusty garb. Lady Sophia—your servant. Mrs Jameson—I do hope your health is improving.'

'Yes, I thank you, sir,' replied Mrs Jameson. 'Oh, yes, indeed it is.'

Lady Sophia's eyes were travelling slowly over

Mr Brand, clearly missing nothing of his well-shaped legs encased in leather boots, the muscles which rippled as he drew down his shirt sleeves and buttoned the cuffs, and the slight tan the sun had given him which made him appear darker and more attractive than ever, and Elinor was assailed by a wave of fury at her ladyship's proprietorial airs.

Mr Brand received her admiring glances without embarrassment and complimented her on her appearance. Lady Sophia knew how to enhance her looks. Her gown was of cream silk and delicate lace, her straw bonnet with celestial blue flowers and feathers framed her face enchantingly, her soft kid gloves encased slim hands. Beneath her gown peeped satin slippers of the exact shade of the adornments on her bonnet and she wore a single strand of tiny pearls. Her outfit was a triumph of taste and Elinor knew instinctively that it had cost as much as, or perhaps more than, her entire fortune.

Lady Sophia held out her hand and automatically Mr Brand offered an arm. He could not ignore Mrs Jameson and she placed her hand upon his other arm. They walked into the drawing-room leaving Elinor to follow alone. It was not her cousin's fault, but Elinor felt unreasonably angry with him.

Nancy brought ratafia, coffee and sweetmeats and Lady Sophia nibbled appreciatively. She was astonished to learn that the chef was a sixteen-year-old girl. 'I never before heard of such a thing. When you set up your establishment properly you will require an experienced cook.'

Mr Brand looked gloomy. 'I begin to doubt my ability to rescue the manor. I have ideas, but . . .'

'What a man in such a position needs is a proper sort of wife,' said Lady Sophia. 'It is something which cannot be argued with.'

Elinor gave a small gasp at her boldness, but perhaps London society was used to such manoeuvres for her cousin simply smiled, as Lady Sophia continued, 'I was saying only a moment ago that the manor could be made beautiful again. Naturally one would have to leave it for the Season and to stay sometimes with friends or travel to foreign parts, but it would be a pretty place in which to relax.'

She accompanied her words with such charming smiles and such laughter in her lovely eyes that Elinor felt like biting a piece from her coffee cup in her fury. It was unfair! An alluring widow, still young, with status and fortune was more than a match for a young girl of modest appearance and no money. Not that it mattered to her, of course! She was not contending for Mr Brand's attention. She simply found it nauseating to see a nice man drawn into the net of a designing female.

She glanced at her cousin to find he was watching her with an expression which made her put down her cup for fear she should spill her coffee. She felt he knew what had been passing through her mind and was amused by her.

He rose and suggested they walk in the garden, where her ladyship and Mrs Jameson were full of praise for the improvements. He looked modestly gratified at their enthusiasm as he bent to point out the beauty of a clump of pinks. Elinor was staring at him and did not notice Bastable's arrival until he spoke so close to her she jumped.

'Beg pardon for interrupting when you've got guests, but can Joe and me take a dressing chest that's got woodworm out of Miss Graham's new bedchamber and put another one in place?'

'My new room!' exclaimed Elinor in such un-guarded surprise that she became the centre of attention.

Bastable put on a chagrined face. 'Oh, sorry, ma'am, I should have waited until Mr Brand was alone to speak—we meant it for a surprise. Now I've spoiled everything.'

'Where is Mrs Tucker putting Miss Graham?' asked Mr Brand.

Elinor felt a suge of irritation. 'I did not request a move,' she protested. 'I think someone might have asked me first.'

Mr Brand looked at her, his brows raised a little. 'You wish to remain in the present bedchamber, Elinor? The plan can easily be altered.'

'I . . . yes . . . no. Oh, do as you will,' she said crossly, then flushed at Lady Sophia's open amusement.

She was about to apologise for her quick temper when Bastable forestalled her. 'We didn't mean to upset you, Miss Graham. Me and Mrs Tucker put it to Mr Brand that you would wish to move after last night and Mr Brand thought it a good idea . . .'

'Last night?' said Lady Sophia sharply.

'Yes, your ladyship. Poor Miss Graham was woke up by . . .'

'Never mind that now,' said Elinor. 'Change my room. It does not signify anyway.'

She might as well not have spoken. Lady Sophia was directing a compelling glance at Bastable, who was happy to oblige. 'Last night Miss Graham thought she heard strange noises. She was so frightened she ran along to Mr Brand's bedchamber. He had to soothe her and then he went to her room, but you didn't hear anything, did you, sir?'

How did he know about her cousin's visit to her room? wondered Elinor. He must have waited and watched in the dark.

The servant would have spoken further but Mr Brand said coolly, 'That will do, Bastable! Elinor, do you wish the servants to move you? It must be your decision.'

Elinor stared angrily at him. He made no effort to explain her conduct of last night. Maybe he believed that the whole episode was a fabrication to gain her admittance to his room? A deep, hot flush rose in a wave of colour over her face and she knew she must look guilty. 'They had as well finish what they have begun,' she said flatly. 'The room is a little large for me anyway.'

Lady Sophia spoke in tones of false jocularity. 'How strange that you should find any room too large! I can never have too much space for my maids to attend me. And of course I need a good dressing-room. It is easy to see you have not lived much in grand houses, Miss Graham.' She plucked a blue flower from a Delphinium plant. 'How pretty these are.'

Elinor felt thankful to have a change of subject, but Lady Sophia had not finished with her. 'What did the servant mean? Do you think Underhill Manor is haunted, Miss Graham? I do not believe in ghosts, do you, Mr Brand?'

Elinor threw him a beseeching look. She knew he

thought her fanciful—or perhaps wanton, she remembered unhappily—but he did not fail her. 'Better men than I have sworn to seeing visions, Lady Sophia.'

Her ladyship's smile was somewhat strained and soon afterwards the guests left and Elinor was able to run upstairs to see where she had been moved. The new room was cosier and furnished with lighter hangings and Elinor liked it better, but she still smarted from her sense of grievance. As soon as she and Nancy were alone she asked, 'Whose idea was it to move me?'

Nancy scratched her head. 'Blest if I know, Miss Elinor. It just seemed to be decided. It's nicer, though, and you've got the same good view over the pleasure grounds.'

Elinor descended the wide stairway and wandered back to the flower garden feeling drained of animation. When she saw her cousin striding along shouldering a hoe, she felt a momentary irritation surpassed swiftly by pleasure.

He sat down, leaning the hoe on the bench and wiped his hands on his waistcoat. 'Phew! Gardening is warm work. I never did any before, but I can understand for the first time the enthusiasm of some of my friends.'

Elinor gave him a cool look. 'You are happy here?'

'It makes a change from London.'

'That is not what I asked.'

'I am happy here, yes. I must say though, Elinor, that you do not appear particularly pleased. It is of no use now to think of the Season. It is almost over! Do you regret coming here?'

'I hardly know what I feel,' she snapped. 'I sense somehow that I am being manipulated—the servants are so odd. Where else would a lady's room be changed without permission?'

'That was explained to you.'

'Evidently you do not find it strange at all.'

Mr Brand's shrug filled her with a longing to stir him. 'Lady Sophia wasted no time in coming into Gloucestershire.'

She felt his intent gaze upon her and would not look when he replied, 'That also was explained.'

'Do you believe in the sudden illness of her aunt? You must be gullible!'

'Society is full of such small evasions of the truth. If you wish to become a London belle you must learn to accept the fact.'

'Or perhaps I should become a repeating parrot like Mrs Jameson.'

She threw a quick glance at her cousin who was leaning back lazily, one arm along the bench, his face humorous. 'An apt description. But one supposes she enjoys her life, else why would she stay?'

'There you go again! You cannot—or will not—comprehend that a woman has almost no choice in her mode of life. I daresay Mrs Jameson is a poor relation. She is glad to chaperone her niece. Lady Sophia needs someone—she is pretty . . .'

She gnawed her lower lip in vexation. Idiot! Idiot to remind her cousin of her ladyship's charms.

'She is lovely,' he agreed, adding in brisker tones, 'and she is to grace our dinner-table a week from today.'

'You have asked her to dine when we are in such a muddle!'

Mr Brand gave it some thought. 'When I escorted her to her carriage she said the manor must look elegant by candlelight and asked if she might drive over some night to see. Somehow that grew into an invitation to dinner.'

'She found it easy to get what she wanted!'

He smiled indulgently. 'She is a woman of the world. Her experience could be useful to you.'

She lashed out in fury. 'What would *she* know of my struggles?'

Her cousin responded quickly. 'Elinor! Does she overset you? I would not like that.'

Elinor revelled in his suddenly caring tones, but forced herself to reply with dignity. 'I have learned more than you might suppose, thank you, and the best I may glean from Lady Sophia is how to cosset a man until he tumbles into my snare.'

Mr Brand's voice was hard. 'And is not that precisely what you wish to know?'

She felt unable to answer and her cousin grasped her arm none too gently. 'Look at me.'

She looked into his eyes which glinted with anger as he repeated his question. 'Yes,' she had to agree, 'that is what I told you.'

She stared into his thin dark features, wishing she could unsay her criticism of Lady Sophia and not have given him the opportunity to reflect that Elinor's motives were worse, having stated her intention to marry a man for his wealth, while her ladyship was prepared to offer her beauty and her money to a man she found attractive.

The pressure from his fingers grew fierce and she jerked her arm and forced him to release her. As soon as she was free she sprang to her feet. 'Pray excuse me, I must prepare Annie for the dinner-party. We must see after provisions . . .'

Annie asked if her mother could come to help at the party and Elinor agreed. 'She may bring others .'

'That won't be needed, miss. We'll manage.'

Elinor was troubled by the girl's obvious nervousness. 'Are you happy here, Annie?'

'That I am, miss. If only my uncle . . .'

She stopped, a hand to her mouth as a shadow fell across the door. Elinor looked up to see Bastable. Annie was trembling.

'Have you no work?' asked Elinor.

The big man strolled across the kitchen with insolent ease. 'Plenty of that, miss. I'm here for a glass of small beer for Mr Brand. He's getting up a powerful thirst out there. And I'd like one, Annie, my girl, so stir yourself.'

The maid scuttled to obey, and Elinor waited while he drank and bore away a brimming tankard. But Annie's confidences were not resumed.

That night, in spite of her pleasant room, Elinor could not sleep. She smoothed her pillows and straightened her sheets as she tried to make sense of her thoughts. Nothing was proceeding according to plan. Was she doomed for ever to be discontented? When the church clock sent out two chimes across the quiet hills she lit a candle and reached for a novel she had borrowed from the Rector's wife. It was not in her bedside cabinet and she padded round the room until the discovery of the book became an obsession. Without it she knew she would not close her eyes that night.

Nancy must have overlooked it in the move, and Elinor was opening her bedchamber door when the memory of the noises in the other room halted her. She closed the door and looked again without success.

'Ghosts!' she declared. 'What nonsense!'

Distance had lent her courage, but as she entered her former room she began to feel weak-kneed. She listened. Nothing! She hurried to the cabinet, opened it and found her book. Her heart was thumping, but not loudly enough to drown the sounds which came abruptly from the wall, and her hand shook so that she spilled hot candle wax on her fingers.

The stab of pain jerked her to a measure of reason. Resolutely she walked to the wall and placed her ear against it. The noises were the same. Should she fetch her cousin? But if he came again to hear nothing he would think her a candidate for Bedlam.

Elinor placed the candle-holder on the mantelpiece and realised that the sounds were louder. They were emanating from the chimney. Did ghosts haunt chimneys?

She tucked her book into her wrapper pocket and walked along the corridor towards the stairway and slowly descended. The tiny candle flame flickered, shadows danced around her and her own grew from dwarf to giant and back.

Downstairs she opened one door after another, but could hear nothing. She stared about the Great Hall and the rusty suits of armour seemed to take on life, and the hollow eyes gleamed momentarily. She was shivering now, but she clung to her nerves.

No one should have the chance to mock her again.

The only place left unexplored was the kitchen, and she pushed her legs in the direction of the door leading to the long corridor. Then, with a suddenness which seemed to stop her heart, the door swung open and a very tall, shapeless white apparition floated out above her head, uttering horrifying moans.

Elinor shrieked and raced for the stairs her feet seeming not to touch the floor and she did not stop running until she reached her bed where she drew the covers over head.

She had left her door open and when a hand closed on her shoulder through the blankets she gave a muffled scream. It was several moments before she realised that her cousin's voice was addressing her in ungentle tones while he shook her.

She threw back the covers and seized his hand between her own. 'Wasn't it awful! Did you hear it? Now you have to believe me!'

He looked around the room in a surprised manner. 'Believe what? I heard you shrieking and found your door open. I knocked several times, but . . .'

His voice trailed away as she clutched convulsively at him. 'I went back to my old room for my book. The noises—they were there. I was afraid no one would believe me—I went downstairs—oh, that awful white thing . . . !

Mr Brand leaned forward to stare into her face. Then he laid his candle on the table and seated himself on her bed. 'Calm down, Elinor. What is it you think you saw?'

'I *know* I saw,' she corrected, her voice quivering. She told him what had happened, endeavouring to keep the panic out of her account, but she saw with a sick feeling that he believed nothing.

She was therefore unsurprised when he said, 'There is nothing in the hall. I could have seen it from the gallery if there had been. My dear, your nerves are overstrained, and it is not surprising . . .'

'They are not! And if they are, it is the fault of your horrid house,' she cried illogically.

'I thought you liked the manor.'

'I do! Well, I like it really—in the daytime I love it—but as soon as darkness falls—why am I the only one to hear what is happening?'

Even in the dim illumination from one candle she could see that he had given her a look of sympathy which bordered on pity, and she was suddenly furious. 'Do not take the trouble to feel sorry for me! I know I am right and—somehow I shall prove it.'

His voice had grown cold. 'On the contrary, I require your promise that you will remain in your bedchamber at nights and not continue to disturb me with your nightmares.'

She realised that she still held his hand and angrily threw it aside with such force that his knuckles rapped on the edge of the table.

'You little vixen . . .' He sucked his raw knuckles.

She was instantly contrite and knelt up in bed, pulling his arm in an attempt to see the damage. 'I did not mean . . .'

He withdrew his hand from his mouth. '*You did not mean* . . . Many are the apologies which begin so. Just what *do* you mean, Elinor, when you bring us together in the middle of the night?'

Surely he did not think she was manufacturing opportunities to be alone with him in the intimacy of darkness? She burned with anger and mortification. At least she tried to assure herself that those were her only emotions, but from deep within her rose a sensation which was terrifying in its weakening power. She knew that this dark closeness was all too sweet.

Without volition her body swayed towards his and her eyes half closed. He caught his breath. 'Elinor, you do not realise . . . for God's sake . . .'

His hands grasped her wrists roughly and he jerked her nearer. She made no attempt to pull away. Indeed, she pushed towards him so that she felt the frogged cords of his dressing gown press painfully into her breasts. Her eyes grew wide as she saw his pupils darken. Their lips joined in a fusion that was lingering, sweet, and shocking in its intensity.

For an eternity Elinor felt the searching mouth on hers and struggled with the power of emotions she could not control. Then she found herself thrust back so hard that she fell across the bed.

'What in hell's name do you think you are doing?' her cousin demanded. 'What kind of woman are you? How often have you played with fire?'

She could do nothing but stare at him, then his fingers touched her bruised lips and his eyes softened. 'Elinor, you are an innocent—a damnably foolish innocent. The sooner you find your rich man and wed him the better for us both.'

He was gone, and she lay for a long time across the bed where he had left her, consumed by an aching longing for something she could not altogether define.

The next morning she half expected him to show the embarrassment she was endeavouring to hide, but he behaved as if the previous night's episode had not occurred. She could only suppose that such nocturnal adventures had been a part of his bachelor life for so long that they were easily put aside. And why not? Society condoned a libertine, but never, she reminded herself painfully, a wanton girl.

They ate breakfast in a silence broken only by Miss Tabitha's artless remarks and Mr Brand rose. 'I have decided to pay a visit to the gipsy encampment. I may discover something about the killing of the man.'

Elinor spoke sharply. 'You will not go alone?'

'Do you think them dangerous?'

'How can I tell? How can you? You should not run risks.'

'Your concern for me is touching, Elinor.'

She looked angrily into his face, but her rage died as she saw that mingled with his sardonic humour was a glint of sadness. She felt a longing to put her arms about him and plead for . . . for what . . .'

'May I come with you?' she begged in a small voice.

'What! You would visit those alarming miscreants?'

She dared not answer. Her wayward tongue might express something which would wipe that curiously caring look from his face. He smiled suddenly. 'All right. I will wait for you to change.'

Feeling ridiculously happy, she raced to her room and put on her midnight blue riding-habit. It had seen two years' wear and was tight in places. In fact, she reflected, looking at herself in the cheval-glass, it gave her a curvaceous appearance which she quite liked.

She was glad to be on horseback again even if the animal was sluggish, and she and her cousin rode through the bright summer morning into the dark heart of the woods where they saw tents, waggons, animals and many barefooted children who ran to stare curiously.

They dismounted and tethered their mounts to a bush and walked into the middle of the camp. A circle of disconcertingly silent men formed about them and Elinor felt nervous and pressed close to her cousin.

With a feeling of relief which she soon realised was unjustified, she saw a face she knew and called, 'Good day, Zenobia! We have met, have we not?'

Zenobia trod forward warily. A wrinkled, bent crone followed her and muttered something. Zenobia spoke soothingly to her. 'Don't worry, Mother. We be more than they.'

'We have come only to talk,' Mr Brand said quietly. 'We have no quarrel with any who are innocent of wrongdoing.'

'Well, that be good of you.' One of the men stepped forward from the ring. He was swarthy of visage and of medium height, yet his thin body gave the impression of wiry animal strength. The other men murmured, and Elinor felt caged by the eyes glowing with suspicion.

She said quickly, 'Zenobia, will you not introduce me to your mother?'

'Mother!' Zenobia threw back her head and gave a harsh laugh. 'I call her Mother because she was to be mine when I wed her son. This be Mazel, queen of our tribe, aye, and many other tribes that wander the west country. It was her son, Luther, that was foully murdered. Him that would have been my husband. My man! My dear man, gone from me for ever!'

Her wail was taken up by the other women and Mazel threw her black skirt over her face and wept aloud. The men drew closer and Elinor tried not to shrink back.

Her cousin showed neither fear nor aggression. He took Elinor's hand and held it, and they remained still until the wails of the women died and there was a silence unbroken even by birds in the dense thickets.

The man who had stepped forward was first to speak. 'What has Zenobia to do with folk from the big house?'

'How do you know where we come from?' Mr Brand countered calmly.

'You watch us; we watch you; fair's fair!'

Zenobia threw the man a fiery glare. 'I can talk for myself, Draco. You don't own me.'

'Not yet!' Draco gave a laugh which made Elinor shiver.

'Not yet, nor never!' cried Zenobia. 'My man be gone, and I'll die a maid.'

Draco moved again until he was insolently close to Mr Brand. 'Go home, gorgio! We don't want your kind here!'

Mr Brand looked past Draco to the gispy queen who was staring at him with coal-black eyes. 'I came to ask your help. One of your number was killed on my land. The guilty should be brought to justice.'

'Leave us be!' Draco's voice was so loud that Elinor jumped.

'Wait!' Mazel hobbled forward, leaning on her stick and the men made way for her. Zenobia flew to her and her voice was tender. 'Careful, Mother. You ain't as strong as you think.' She gave Draco a defiant look. 'Mazel speaks for us, not you.' The toss of her head caught a filtered beam of light and turned her hair to shining jet.

Mazel stood close to Mr Brand and one claw-like hand touched his face. 'I see you be good. Thank you for your favour, but we've got our own justice. We shall discover the wicked and punish them.'

Not another word could be got from the gipsies. Even Draco remained silent, though his eyes moved watchfully.

As they left the encampment Mr Brand expelled a long breath. 'What an atmosphere! What people! Elinor, almost I could accept your description of our surroundings as sinister.'

But he was teasing her, and Elinor set her lips and tried to urge her nag into a trot, failed, and was forced to remain by her cousin, maintaining an indignant silence.

The next few days were taken up in receiving callers and paying return visits. Elinor, Miss Tabitha and Mr Brand drove from gracious homes to houses where hearty squires presided over robust families. They travelled across rolling, fertile country to grey stone farms which had crouched for centuries on the earth which supported their owners. Everywhere they were received with courtesy, but their pleasure was eroded in concern for the folk who dwelled on Underhill estates in cottages and smallholdings which were decrepit and barren. And they found it difficult to uphold a semblance of tranquillity when they were stared at with sullen anger by men and women who were thin and ragged and who held their pale-faced children close to their sides as they passed.

'The results of the years of neglect,' muttered Mr Brand. 'I wish I could do something to help. I shall try. I have learned that my land is mostly hill country and poor—what is needed is a good breed of sheep. The flocks are full of disease and have not the qualities needed for surviving and producing healthy lambs.'

When Mr Brand tried to raise the subject of the gipsy's murder with the local men he found they were interested in the robberies only and he elicited nothing further. The Underhill party made so many new acquaintances that it was decided to forgo the dinner for a *soirée* that all could attend, and Elinor tried not to feel a vengeful pleasure at Lady Sophia's ill-concealed annoyance when she realised that there was to be no small, intimate evening.

CHAPTER
SEVEN

THE gentlefolk arrived in their dozens. The large reception room had been opened up and cleaned, and Annie and her mother had managed to prepare a surprising number of delicacies. Even Tucker had remembered some Chinese lanterns long abandoned in the attic, and surprised everyone by stringing them in the trees, and a tuner was brought from Stow-on-the-Wold to restore the old pianoforte to melodious tones.

The manor was festive with talking, laughter and food, and Mr Brand was besieged by advisers anxious to tell him how best to tackle the problem of his land.

'And tackled it must be,' pronounced Sir Henry. 'It is disastrous for a man's neighbours when a place is allowed to go to ruin.'

Lady Barnwall spoke across the room. 'Indeed it is. My husband is for ever having to sentence poachers who have increased in number. When a landowner has no gamekeepers . . .'

'It is disgraceful,' said an elderly dowager who had accompanied two blushing young ladies. 'Such folk seem to have no respect for righteousness.'

'But the game laws are harsh!' exclaimed Elinor. 'If a man sees his family hungry. . . !'

The dowager lifted her eyeglass and gave Elinor a frown. 'You are not one of those dreadful bluestocking women, are you?'

Elinor glanced over in her cousin's direction, but he had been monopolised again by the men, and she was nervous beneath the haughtily enquiring looks of several of the older women.

'Miss Graham has only just left school,' said a voice she knew. Lady Sophia was moving gracefully, her gown of pale green silk a miracle of perfection.

'That explains something, I suppose,' admitted the dowager. 'Though I shudder at the idea of your parents sending you to a seminary of such radical notions.'

'Miss Brown was not radical, ma'am. I know people should not steal, but . . .'

'Give a labourer an inch and he will take a mile,' the dowager stated firmly. 'Would you have us uncomplaining about the loss of our family treasures?'

'No . . . no, of course not . . .' Elinor stammered. 'It is just that taking a little food from the land seems scarcely a crime to me.'

'It is easy to see that Miss Graham has lived most of her life abroad and has never settled long in one place,' remarked Lady Sophia, seating herself on a satin couch.

'Oh!' The dowager surveyed Elinor through her eye-glass once more. 'That explains it. Well, now you are in Britain, miss, and must conform to *our* standards.'

Elinor was bereft of words. It had occurred to her rather belatedly that whatever her sentiments, she should not argue with her cousin's guests. She felt exposed and vulnerable, and when Lady Sophia patted a vacant place beside her she sank into it. Her ladyship spoke close to her ear. 'Your compassion does you credit, but your cousin would not wish you to be at outs with his neighbours.'

Elinor could not quarrel with a thought which echoed her own, and she was forced to clasp her hands and remain silent.

Mr Brand had escaped at last from the questions of the male visitors, and approached them carrying two glasses of iced champagne. 'Good evening, Lady Sophia. You look hot, Elinor. This should refresh you.'

Lady Sophia laughed at him over the rim of her glass. 'Your little cousin has been alarming the dowagers by her radical opinions!'

'Elinor? Radical? What can you have been saying? Was it something to do with the inferior position of ladies in this imperfect world?'

'Now that is an interesting notion,' declared Lady Sophia. 'Does Miss Graham champion not only the morally weak, but also our poor downtrodden sex?'

Mr Brand bowed, laughing down at her ladyship. 'Anyone less downtrodden than yourself would be difficult to find.'

Lady Sophia acknowledged his speech with a pout. 'You will not accuse me of outrageous ideals, I hope.'

'Is that how you see me?' demanded Elinor. 'As outrageous?'

She spoke to Lady Sophia, but she stared at her cousin, who frowned slightly. Before he could speak Lady Sophia said softly, 'Pray moderate your tone, my dear Miss Graham, or you will have the old ladies down on you again. They are staring your way.'

Elinor relapsed into a silent fury which was increased when Lady Sophia said, 'Mr Brand I find the evening sultry and the room a trifle warm. Will you not escort me into the garden? I am sure your guests can spare you for a while. Miss Graham can keep them amused, can you not?'

Her ladyship's green eyes flashed into Elinor's with more than a hint of malicious enjoyment which turned to triumph as Mr Brand held out a black-sleeved arm for her hand and they stepped through the open, floor-level windows leading to the garden.

Elinor found it almost impossible to tear her imagination from the two of them out among the Chinese lanterns. The breeze would ruffle Lady Sophia's expertly-dressed dark hair and whisper through her silken gown. How could a man resist her? Why should Mr Brand in particular *want* to resist a woman who could give him everything? If he must marry, then her ladyship was the obvious choice.

She circulated among the guests, paying particular attention to the dowagers she had offended in an effort to eradicate their first impression. The sound of a pianoforte being played at the end of the reception room turned all heads in the direction of Miss Tabitha, who was seated at the instrument and allowing her fingers to play with the strains of a country dance.

A murmur of pleasure ran through the younger

folk and sets began to form. Elinor longed for Mr
Brand to come to her side and lead her into the
dance, and chagrin welled into her throat when she
saw her cousin and Lady Sophia hurry into the
room as a summer shower filled the night with a
haunting scent of damp foliage and earth, and walk
straight to a set.

Mr Robinson's curate asked if he might dance
with her. When she hesitated he glanced at her
black gloves. 'A country dance in your own home
could not be considered wrong.'

Her feet tapped. 'Just one, then,' she conceded,
and she allowed Mr Hawkins to escort her to make
up an eight for Mall Peatly. It did not help her to
control her warring emotions when she saw that
Lady Sophia and Mr Brand were members of the
same set, and that during the weaving pattern of the
steps her ladyship flirted with Mr Brand in a manner
which would have been unseemly if conducted by
an unwed girl.

She went back to the dowagers when the music
ended and worked so hard at creating a good impression that she was pronounced a nice gel with
pretty manners. The small accolade was almost lost
as Lady Sophia could clearly be heard saying petu-
lantly, 'Oh, come, Miss Tabitha, do not be fustian!
Society no longer frowns on it. It is even danced at
Almacks by permission of the Patronesses. I have
taken part there myself.'

Miss Tabitha was close to tears and wringing her
hands, and as a hush fell upon the room her voice
was audible as she protested timidly, but firmly,
'Dear Lady Sophia, please forgive me, but I cannot
play for you to dance the waltz. My late papa, the

curate, was shocked to learn of it. I have no wish to offend you.'

'Indeed!' Her ladyship's tones were chilling. 'Well, I consider your criticism of me to be quite indefensible.'

'But I am not criticising you. It is only that the waltz . . .'

Elinor began to move to the pianoforte, uncertain what to do, but drawn by the embarrassment of the governess. Before she reached her the problem was solved when Mrs Jameson offered to play and Miss Tabitha hurried away, her cheeks scarlet.

Mr Brand also moved to be near the distressed governess and consequently was at Lady Sophia's side when the piano playing recommenced. In a moment she had curtsied low and said, 'Come, sir, you must know the steps. Pray help me to lead the way.'

He could not be blamed for conducting her on to the centre of the floor where his arm encircled her waist in so intimate a gesture that several girls new from the schoolroom gasped.

They began to circle the floor, their bodies moving in unison and her ladyship threw back her head and smiled dazzlingly.

To Elinor the waltz seemed to last for ever, then the dowagers decided that the evening should end and began to shepherd their charges towards their cloaks and carriages. Elinor blamed her ladyship for the break-up of the party and found it difficult to say goodnight civilly to her.

In a short time the room was empty of all but Tucker and Nancy, who went round snuffing out the candles. Elinor leaned her head on the cool

window-pane and stared out at the trees which
soughed in the wind and showered droplets. Deep
within her she felt a slow burning as she thought of
the events of the evening.

She remembered her cousin's arm about Lady
Sophia and emotion rose like gall in her throat.
Jealousy! She was jealous! Without right or encour-
agement she was bitterly envious of the attraction
which her ladyship must hold for Mr Brand. There
was a sharp pain in her as she thought suddenly, *I
want to be where she was.* She longed to be held by
him; not in only physical desire, not in abortive
passion born of proximity in the darkness of her
night terrors, but in public, openly, without the
need for shame.

She realised with abrupt clarity that she loved
him. When had it happened? How? She could not
tell, but once admitted she realised that she had
wanted him, loved him, from their first meeting.

She was aware that the servants had finished as
Nancy placed a candle near her and said she would
wait upstairs to help her undress. Elinor remained
motionless until she heard a soft footfall and Mr
Brand asked, 'Are you all right, Elinor?'

'Why should I not be?'

Despair sharpened her voice. She heard a slight
intake of his breath and wanted to beat her
clenched fists into the window glass. *Of course I am
not all right. I love you, and it is no use. You do not
care for me.*

She turned to face him, twisting the knife in her
wounded heart. 'Lady Sophia looked particularly
beautiful, I thought.'

His raised brows expressed his surprise. 'She did

indeed. I did not think you had much love for her.'

'One can admire a thing of beauty without particularly liking it.'

'You are ungenerous! She never says anything unkind about you. In fact, she is always quick to praise.'

Quick to place me firmly back where she wants me to belong, raged Elinor inwardly, *down with the young women fresh from the schoolroom, while she . . . she is a lady of consequence and wealth who can satisfy all your needs.*

She was saved from a reply by Bastable who entered the room with muffled tread. 'The bolts are in place, sir. Is there anything else you need?'

'No, thank you. The servants did well tonight.'

He touched his forelock in his deliberately subservient way. 'We'm all glad to be of service, sir.'

Bastable's tone, his leer, his general air of suppressed aggression all added to Elinor's fury. Or perhaps the memory of Lady Sophia in Mr Brand's arms was enblazoned too painfully into her brain for rationality. She walked swiftly from the room and was on the half-landing before her cousin caught her up.

He had mounted the stairs two or three at a time and was breathing hard. 'Such haste, Elinor. Are you so tired?'

'A little,' she said shortly.

'So am I. Physical labour goes ill with late nights. And I need my sleep, especially tonight, because . . .'

'I am sure you do. I fear *you* must be quite worn out by your evening's activities.'

Mr Brand's brows rose. 'Have I upset you in some way?'

'You? Certainly not! How should you?'

'I do not know, but I am sure you are angry with me.'

'All right, yes I am! I think it is the outside of enough for Lady Sophia to tell me I must be circumspect in my behaviour so as not to antagonise the local gentlefolk, then order a waltz to be danced in another's home! And you encouraged her by leading her in the dance when you must have been aware of the nature of some of your guests' feelings!'

His brows drew close above angry eyes. 'That is unfair, and you must know it. I had no choice. How could I insult her by rejecting her invitation while all the guests were watching?'

The fact that he was right added fuel to the flames of Elinor's fury. 'Oh, it is easy enough to make excuses. If you had been truly desirous of preventing the dance you would have found a way. Perhaps you wished to hold Lady Sophia . . .' her voice faltered at the sudden look in her cousin's eyes, but she forced herself to finish, ' . . . in close contact.'

His rage was almost tangible as he took a step nearer and she moved back summoning all her resolve to return his glare. 'How dare you presume to speak to me like that, madam! To insinuate that I am so lost to propriety as to permit a waltz so that I might have an opportunity to embrace someone!'

Elinor was now hard-pressed against the wall and still Mr Brand moved nearer. As she struggled to find words to placate him she became afraid of his blazing fury. She tried to look away, but he seized her chin and forced her to face him. 'Have I given you cause to doubt my honour?'

Words were ground out of her by jealousy. 'You were quick to hold *me* close.'

Her voice cracked as the grip on her chin tightened. His reply was delivered icily and brought the shamed blood to her face. 'You came to *my* room, Elinor, and on the second occasion your shrieks drew me to *you*.'

Tears stung her eyes. 'You think me shameless!' she stormed.

He released her abruptly. 'No!'

She scarcely heard him. It seemed that she would appear wrong whatever she did, and her need tore through her. 'If I am to be judged I may as well commit the crime.'

She threw herself at him so violently that he almost staggered. His arms came up to steady himself and remained about her shaking form as she lifted herself on tiptoe and pressed her mouth full on his. For an instant he stiffened, held her arms as if to repulse her, then began to return her kiss with an abandon which matched her own. Her blood coursed through her veins as she pulled his head closer.

It was like a physical blow when he groaned and dragged her arms from him and pushed her back with such force that she hit the wall.

'My God, Elinor! You play dangerous games!'

Games! He thought she was amusing herself. She put a hand to her bruised lips and sick shame invaded her. 'I suppose all love-making is a game to you,' she cried. 'Well, you should know. I daresay you have had plenty of practice.'

The rage in his eyes sent her running up the stairs and he did not follow her. 'Damn you, Christopher

Brand! Damn you!' she muttered as she slammed her bedchamber door.

Even in her room she was denied the relief of weeping. Nancy was waiting. She had placed pails to catch water drips from the ceiling. 'The sooner Mr Brand mends the roof the better, Miss Elinor.'

Once in bed Elinor could not sleep as mental images tormented her. She saw Mr Brand wedded to Lady Sophia, who would play her rôle beautifully, ministering to the villagers until she wearied of the charade. Lady Sophia chaperoning her into society. The latter idea made Elinor sit up, her heart thumping. Sooner would she return to Miss Brown's Academy.

'It isn't fair!' she exclaimed as she beat her hot pillow.

Her cousin could not be blamed for marrying a rich woman. Everywhere he turned, people were waiting for help. A rumble of thunder and a flash of lightning sent her to the window. Without air she would surely suffocate. As she opened her casement a second flash lit up two figures who were carrying large bags from the house.

Robbers! She must tell her cousin. She had taken a step to the door when she was stopped by the memory of his accusations. By the time she got to him the men would have vanished. Then what? More sarcasm? Another sheet of lightning revealed that one of the men was Bastable, who probably had nothing more sinister on his mind than poaching, and, glad that she had not made a fool of herself, Elinor climbed back into her bed.

*   *   *

She woke when Nancy carried in a tray. 'I looked in an hour ago, but you were still sleeping.'

Elinor drank her tea quickly and fidgetted as Nancy buttoned her into a silver-grey muslin. Her humiliation of the night before was still so vivid that her nerves shook at the idea of confronting her cousin, but she must try to eradicate the false impression.

Forcing her tones to casualness she asked, 'Has Mr Brand been up long? Is he gardening?'

Nancy was astonished. 'Fancy you not knowing! Everyone else does.'

'Knowing what?'

'That the master's gone on a visit to a friend in Norfolk.'

'What? You are mistaken!'

Elinor stopped, warned by the maid's surprise. She wanted no gossip. She held out her foot for Nancy to tie the ribbon of her kid pump. 'I recall that Mr Brand tried to tell me something yesterday. We were interrupted.' Interrupted by her own uncontrolled outburst, she thought bitterly. 'I daresay he will soon return,' she finished carefully.

'I don't know. Tucker says a letter came yesterday in answer to one that was sent to his friend. The master's bags were packed for an indefinite stay.'

It was a terrible effort to sound normal. 'Have you plenty to do, Nancy?'

'That I have. After the clearing up I'm going to take down curtains and lay them in the sun. They're too old to stand washing.'

As Nancy was leaving Elinor could not resist asking, 'Did . . . was the purpose of Mr Brand's visit mentioned?'

'It seems that Mr Coke, the gentleman in Norfolk, was a friend of the master's late father, and Mr Brand goes every year for the shooting and other sports.'

Elinor paced her room, resentment growing like a canker. He had been so full of talk of reform, and had simply abandoned everything and gone off on a pleasure trip. How double-faced of him! She ached to be able to tell him her opinion. Then her anger gave way to misery as she faced the fact that without him her life was savourless.

Her outrage was a little mitigated when Miss Tabitha handed her a note. 'Dear Mr Brand,' she enthused. 'He came to me early and asked me to give you this. He would not disturb you. How considerate he is!'

The note was disappointingly brief. It informed Elinor that her cousin had gone into Norfolk. He hoped she kept well in his absence.

Elinor's lacerated feelings needed air and solitude. In the garden, walking along the gravelled paths between newly-weeded flower beds, she began to pray that she would conquer a love which was agonising because it was unreturned.

She blinked moisture from her eyes, despising herself for her weakness. A moment later she was thankful she had not given way as she saw Lady Sophia walking towards her.

'Good morning,' cried her ladyship gaily. 'I would not allow your servant to precede me.'

Her ladyship looked lovely in pale yellow silk and a chip-straw hat and her next words struck at Elinor's self-control. 'I have come to offer you amusement in the absence of Mr Brand.'

Elinor was not clever enough to hide her shock, and Lady Sophia's tones became chidingly benevolent. 'Never say he forgot to tell you he was going away!'

'He did *not* forget. We were too busy to talk and he left a note.'

'That is all right then,' soothed Lady Sophia. 'I have come to ask for your company on a little outing, just you and I. We can drive down the valley to the River Windrush and eat *al fresco*. Do you say you will come. I want to know you better.'

The last thing Elinor felt like doing was going on a trip with Lady Sophia, and she was trying to think of an excuse when her ladyship said, 'There is a matter we must discuss. I have left my aunt at home in order that we may be entirely private.'

Shortly afterwards Elinor was seated in her ladyship's elegant open carriage, holding an ancient parasol of rather rusty black discovered by Nancy in a cupboard and hastily brushed. Behind them drove a second carriage with servants and hampers.

Lady Sophia, looking coolly beautiful and in command of herself and her situation, was exuding an air of pleased anticipation which gave Elinor an uneasy sensation of dread.

CHAPTER
EIGHT

At first Elinor could take no exception to Lady Sophia's conduct as a delicious meal was served on the banks of the clear trout stream. While the servants cleared, she and her ladyship strolled beneath the willows and smiled at the fish as they leaped for hovering insects.

Then Lady Sophia said, an edge to her voice, 'You are fond of your cousin, are you not?'

Elinor answered levelly, 'I am indeed, though he is not closely related. He is a distant cousin.'

'You speak as if that mattered.'

Elinor managed an amused laugh. 'I know all the relationships in my family. When I was a child my papa told me often of England, and it interested me to study our family tree.'

'I see. Do forgive me, Miss Graham, but I must speak to you. You are young and without womanly advice.'

'You sound as if you are about to lecture me.'

'Be serious, my child . . .'

'I am *not* a child!'

Lady Sophia placed a gentle hand on Elinor's arm. 'A *mature* woman endeavours to remain calm in all circumstances.'

Elinor stifled an impulse to shout at her ladyship

to come to the point, but she needed no such instruction. 'Miss Graham, I cannot help thinking you have hopes in Mr Brand's direction.'

She ignored Elinor's indignant glance. 'I must make matters clear. I have been acquainted with your cousin for many years—ever since my Comeout. He has been the despair of all aspiring mammas who would be content to wed their moneyed daughters to such a handsome man of good breeding.'

Elinor kept her eyes on the river. A fish darted to the surface and ripples disturbed the surface. Words are like that, she thought. She is going to tell me something that will alter my whole life.

Lady Sophia continued: 'When Mr Brand inherited Jonas Webb's property everyone expected him to sell to anyone who would remove the burden. I am amazed to see how deeply he has involved himself. I begin to believe that he intends to remain and set the manor to rights. He seems to care for the people.'

'He still has some power to surprise you,' remarked Elinor. 'After such long friendship surely you know everything about him.'

Lady Sophia's laugh was gently superior. 'It is interesting when friends can disconcert one, is it not?'

Elinor stopped and stared into Lady Sophia's eyes, catching a glimpse of irritation which gave her a sense of satisfaction. 'Did you bring me here to tell me what I already know?'

'So impetuous! I thought it best to make our relationship plain to you, Miss Graham. Mr Brand needs substantial help if he is to realise his ambitions. Help which you cannot give him, but which I can.'

'Has he asked you for assistance?' Elinor's question was restrained, though she dreaded the reply.

'Of course he has not! Would he be so crude? But he has no illusions about money—why should he have? He is a man of the world.'

It was true, and Elinor could not deny it.

Her ladyship went on, 'So you see, Miss Graham, you must allow your cousin to take the way which is best for him. Oh, I will not deny that you have an advantage in sharing his house. An *unscrupulous* girl might feel tempted to use such advantage to— attract—a man.' The laugh trilled again. 'He is, after all, used to gaining his way with the ladies. Men are such vulnerable creatures, are they not?'

Colour flared in Elinor's face. 'Has my cousin offered for you, ma'am?'

'Really! It is not at all the thing to be so direct! But I forgive you! You have lacked guidance.'

'Papa . . .' began Elinor furiously. She stopped. She would not exchange words with this superior creature about her father. 'I thought you wished to clarify things.'

'Indeed, I do, but there are certain—delicate subjects which should be allowed to flower naturally. I felt it my duty to give you a friendly warning and can tell you, in confidence, of course, that I have both authority and reason for asserting that a firm understanding lies between your cousin and myself.'

Elinor turned away, misery engulfing her. She had lost a battle which she had not even realised had been joined.

The drive back passed almost in silence. Elinor longed for solitude, but it was denied her. As the carriage bowled up the drive Lady Sophia touched her arm.

'Miss Graham, you have visitors. Heavens! What a motley collection!'

Elinor gained a general impression of a tattered berline coach laden with portmanteaux and bandboxes, and several people, not one of whom she knew.

She found the patronising amusement of Lady Sophia's face unbearable and scarcely waited for the steps before she leapt down and hurried to the arrivals. She was brought up short by a woman who was directing operations in a mixture of French and English, and who rose to her diminutive height of something over five feet. She revealed a face in which solemnity warred with a dimpled smile.

Elinor asked, 'Are you guests of my cousin?'

The lady exclaimed, 'So you are Elinor! After so long apart, to see you again! What joy!'

Elinor gasped. Her brain reeled beneath a suspicion which was confirmed.

'You do not know me, do you, and why should you, but when I look into your eyes I see myself when young.'

'M . . . Mamma . . . !'

'At last!' Mrs Graham threw out her arms theatrically. Elinor could not move. She had viewed her mother through her father's eyes as a fragile moth burned by flying too close to the flame of life. This sudden transition into a flesh-and-blood woman with golden hair streaked with grey and a somewhat brittle voice held her fast. A woman, moreover, who apparently intended to make herself at home in Underhill Manor during the absence of its owner. Another score for Lady Sophia!

Elinor glanced uncertainly at her ladyship, who was being handed down by her footman. She strolled to the berline. 'Will you introduce us, Miss Graham?'

'My . . . Mrs Marianne Graham—Lady Sophia Deane,' stammered Elinor.

'You are related?'

Mrs Graham rose from her curtsey. 'I am her mother.'

'How very—interesting! We have never met!'

'I have lived out of England for years. In France, mostly.'

'Ah! Such an amusing country. The fashions! *Quelle élégance*!'

Her eyes flickered over Mrs Graham's pelisse of last year's style, the bonnet with jaded roses and the patched gloves. 'You are planning to stay?'

'Indeed I am! I so long to renew my daughter's acquaintance. As Mr Brand is our relative I came here straight from the crossing.'

Lady Sophia laughed unmirthfully. 'I will leave you, Miss Graham, to your guests.'

She gave a last glance at the tatterdemalion group, climbed into her carriage and departed with a wave. Elinor watched her, knowing that as soon as she arrived home Mrs Jameson, who was of an age to recall old scandals, would resurrect all the memories of the shocking behaviour of Mrs Graham. By tomorrow the entire neighbourhood would know that a lady who was said to have absconded from her husband with an Earl had taken up residence in Underhill Manor, without an invitation from Mr Brand.

Elinor managed to extend a welcoming hand to her mother before hurrying in to get assistance with the luggage. As she reached the front door she was amazed to hear a youthful voice call, 'Where are we, Tante Marianne? Have we arrived?'

She whirled to see a tousled, black curly head emerge from the carriage window. An elderly maid bearing the unmistakable signs of an Ancient Retainer appeared from the other side of the carriage.

'So you are awake, Master Dominic! The sooner we find the nursery, the sooner you can bathe and change.'

Elinor felt even more harassed as Bastable appeared and began to lift down the heavy trunks, looking evil-tempered, while the child darted around asking questions and disregarding his nurse's commands.

Joe appeared and Elinor asked him to find Nancy. Bastable glared at her.

'T'aint no use expecting her to help. She's had an accident. Her ankle's hurt.'

He paid no attention to Elinor's exclamations and questions, and asked one of his own.

'Will the visitors be staying long?'

'What is it to do with you?'

'We've got enough to do without opening more rooms.'

'Where is Nancy?' asked Elinor, biting her lip with vexation. If Mr Brand had been here, Bastable would not have spoken to her in such a way.

'She's in her bed, and Miss Tabitha's been looking after her.'

Elinor left clear instructions that her mother and her party were to be comfortably accommodated before going to her maid. Nancy was sitting in an armchair, a defiant look on her homely face. 'I've refused to go to bed,' she declared. 'I don't trust anyone round here except you, Miss Elinor.'

'Oh, be reasonable, Nancy. An accident! That can happen to anyone.'

Nancy snorted. 'It wasn't no accident. Bastable was holding the ladder while I reached for the curtains, and he deliberately let go when I was leaning over. I could have been killed.'

'I cannot believe he would do anything so bad. He could not wish to harm you. Why should he?'

'That I can't tell you, but if I hadn't landed on a pile of cushions I might not have been here to tell you the tale.'

Elinor stared at her maid helplessly. 'But there is no reason for Bastable to injure you.'

Nancy set her lips and Elinor said, 'Say nothing more until we see Mr Brand.'

'Huh! What makes you think he'll listen? He didn't believe you when you heard funny noises!'

'How do you know?'

Nancy stuck out her lower lip. 'Bastable told us he'd found you outside the master's door. Betsy sniggered.'

Elinor's face was scarlet. 'Only Betsy?'

'Yes. Annie and the Tuckers looked terrified. It's my belief there's something mighty peculiar going on here.'

Elinor tried hard to come to terms with the fact that the little woman who fluttered about like a sparrow was her mother. That night, at dinner, she watched Miss Tabitha struggling to accept the presence of a sinful woman whom she regarded as she might a wild beast who could attack her at any moment. Once, Elinor caught Bastable's eye fixed on them with such loathing that it seemed as if Nancy could be right. It was not surprising that she found herself with a headache, and decided to follow her mother's example and retire early.

She was preparing for bed when an altercation outside her door sent her to investigate. Dominic was trying to hide in the folds of his nurse's skirt as Bastable came pounding along the corridor shaking his fist.

'Limb o' Satan!' he yelled. 'Keep out of my quarters or it'll be the worse for you!'

Elinor glared. 'Stop shouting at him. What has he done?'

The boy began to jabber in French and was shaken by the maid. 'Talk God's own language, if you please. We're not with the Frenchies now, heaven be praised!'

'I wanted something to eat,' said Dominic. 'That man—he tried to hit me.'

'And I will, if you come prying in the kitchen again!'

'You will do no such thing,' declared Elinor, placing herself between the boy and Bastable, who had stepped nearer. 'I have yet to learn that a child may not beg dainties from the cook.'

Bastable's touch of his forehead was a masterpiece of an insult. 'Beggin' your pardon, miss, I'm sure. We'll have to see what the master says about this little lot, won't we?'

He stumped off. Elinor felt angry and ill as the throbbing in her temples increased. The nurse looked closely at her. 'May I come to you later?'

Too drained to argue, Elinor nodded, and half an hour later the maid was leaning over her bed, expert hands massaging the pain away. 'I knew you had the headache as soon as I looked at you. I was maid to your blessed grandmother and nurse to Miss Marianne. When my young mistress ran from your papa I had to choose between you and her.' The strong old fingers seemed to gauge the pain areas exactly. 'Your grandmother had headaches like these. It fair broke my heart to leave you, but your pa was good. I knew he'd look after you, while your ma has no more sense than a babe.'

Next morning Miss Tabitha was full of agitation. 'Fancy Cousin Marianne arriving! I wonder if folk will call. What will Cousin Christopher say?'

Visitors were quick to arrive, and by the time Lady Sophia and Mrs Jameson called Elinor had been reassured by her mother's behaviour, which was impeccable. Even her ladyship's gentle-seeming, but caustic comments failed to provoke her, and Lady Sophia took a cake and sank her sharp white teeth into it. Then shouting was heard from the garden and a small figure charged through the long window, tripped over Miss Tabitha's feet and sprawled in front of her ladyship. Muddy hands grasped her pale rose gown, which was further spoiled as she slopped her tea.

She gave a piercing shriek as she deplored the ruination of her gown. 'Silk, newly arrived from Paris!' she cried. 'Who on earth is this?'

'My mother's ward,' replied Elinor briefly, despatching Annie to the kitchen for damp cloths.

Dominic rose and looked around defiantly. 'That man tried to hit me again.'

The Rector's wife looked amused. 'Small boys sometimes need chastising. What have you done?'

'Nothing!'

Mrs Graham waved a white hand towards the door. 'Dominic, *mon petit*, go and wash.'

Lady Sophia was watching carefully, her gown forgotten. 'Ward, did you say? Is he a relative?'

'I chanced upon him in Palermo,' answered Mrs Graham quietly. 'He has no one else.'

'How very generous of you! If a trifle eccentric! I cannot think I would follow your example.'

Mrs Robinson ignored this remark and suggested to Mrs Graham that Dominic might care to join her family in the Parsonage for lessons.

Dominic stared at her. 'Me, I do not like lessons, but I like *you*, and I will come.'

'And you will be safe from Bastable,' said Mrs Robinson.

'I only took a few apricot tarts,' grumbled Dominic.

Lady Sophia suddenly tired of the conversation. She moved so abruptly that Annie, who was on her knees trying to sponge away the marks on her gown, almost toppled sideways. 'It will be a good thing when Mr Brand returns. He is needed to sort out these—complications.'

Lady Barnwall passed her in the doorway. She was full of chatter about the latest robbery which had taken place ten miles away. She said that a substantial reward had been offered for the apprehension of the villains. Dominic's eyes gleamed.

'Someone will pay to get their silver back?'

His remark was unheeded, and Elinor was glad that Nurse hurried in to remove her charge. He was taken the next day to the Robinson's schoolroom and Nurse declared his bedchamber damp and insisted on removing his things to Elinor's former room, completely disregarding the loud protests from Bastable.

Elinor began to wonder if Mr Brand would absent himself for the whole sun-filled summer. A letter gave her little consolation. It said simply that he was enjoying his stay, hoped that the occupants of the manor were well and looked forward to seeing them on his return. He remained her Obedient and Affectionate Cousin.

Elinor tore the letter to bits and hurled them to the floor, then spent the next hour trying to fit them together again. She was relieved that rules of etiquette precluded correspondence between Lady Sophia and Mr Brand. She would prefer to be present when he learned of her mother's arrival.

She wandered into the garden and came upon Jacky, the gipsy boy, staring up at the branches of a cherry tree. Dominic was there, the bough bent beneath his weight as he picked bunches of cherries and threw them down. He grinned and threw Elinor a luscious handful. She retreated into the shade, munching appreciatively, and Bastable did not notice her when he stumped into view.

He glared. 'What you boys doing?' He caught sight of Elinor and said, 'That fruit might be wanted for the table.'

'There is plenty,' replied Elinor coolly.

From the safety of height Dominic directed a

triumphant smile on the servant who stared back angrily.

'Have you nothing to do?' asked Elinor.

'There's always too much,' he growled.

'When you have time to spare I wish to have the bakehouse unblocked.' She stopped speaking as her breathing became uneven from the pounding of her heart. Bastable's look was so malevolent that she stepped back.

'The master didn't give orders about that!'

'He left me in charge, and that is what I want.'

The man stayed motionless, and as if mesmerised by his hostility Elinor and boys did not move. Elinor was first to break free. She looked at Dominic, whose glittering eyes were fixed on the servant. He was holding excitement in check.

Bastable said slowly, 'I'll do it when I've got the time.'

He sloped off and Elinor shivered. When Mr Brand returned she would be glad to hand back the management of the manor. When he returned!

Dominic leaped to the ground and jerked his thumb at Bastable's back. 'He was in a rage, no?'

Elinor nodded before turning to Jacky. 'Is your sister well?'

Jacky looked frightened and ran from her, his bare brown feet seeming not to notice the sharpness of the gravel walk.

'Are you sleeping well?' Elinor asked Dominic.

He looked wary. 'What do you mean?'

His manner was a little too deferential, and Elinor took his shoulder and gave it a small shake. 'Nothing has disturbed you? You are comfortable at night?'

Dominic's strong white teeth gleamed in a cheeky grin. 'You are remembering the ghosts! The servants talk of ghosts!' He jerked himself free and sprang out of reach. His voice shrilled out. 'I like the room better than any I ever had.'

Elinor watched his flying figure and was startled when Bastable rose from behind some currant bushes. They were neglected and barren, and she knew he had been spying on her.

Nothing significant had been said, she decided, but as Bastable threw her a look of loathing and stumped off she felt uneasy and nervous.

CHAPTER
NINE

ELINOR returned to the house, which felt empty of
late, and joined her mother and Miss Tabitha in the
small drawing-room where she sat on a low stool,
chin in her hands. When the door opened and
Annie burst in she almost toppled.

The maid was distraught. 'Oh, come quick! It's
Nancy!'

Elinor beat Annie to the kitchen. She had had
some idea of Nancy being attacked by Bastable and
was startled to find her rigid against the large
cupboard, staring at Bastable's lurcher dog which
crouched, slavering and growling, its hackles brist-
ling, its yellow teeth bared in a vicious snarl.

'I was going to clean the cupboard,' hissed
Nancy, 'and this brute went for me.'

'Get your uncle!' snapped Elinor to Annie.

The maid seemed unable to move as Nancy
shifted her weight to ease her painful ankle and the
dog's lips curled back from its fangs.

Elinor said urgently, 'Annie, where is Bastable?'

'I . . . I don't know.'

Elinor was positive she was lying, but Nancy was
beginning to look exhausted and, setting her face,
she picked up a heavy skillet and advanced on the
dog as Miss Tabitha and Mrs Graham came panting
into the kitchen.

They made small noises of horrified protest as they watched. Nancy, now extremely pale, began to sway in a half-swoon. The dog was going for her throat. Elinor sprang forward, but she was passed by someone who moved with lightning speed, the dog was gripped by its rope collar and a strong hand twisted until the dripping jaws opened in gasping helplessness.

'Cousin Christopher!' breathed Elinor. 'Oh, thank God!'

The dog gradually stopped its jerking attempts to escape and lay at Mr Brand's feet. He stared down at it for a moment. 'I hate to hurt an animal. Its master is the one who should suffer.'

He helped Nancy to a chair and the Tuckers crept out from the pantry, Tucker carrying brandy which was held to the maid's lips. Her colour was restored and she attempted to rise and walk.

'You are limping,' said Mr Brand. 'Did the dog bite you?'

Everyone spoke at once in an effort to tell him of Nancy's accident, and as he tried to sort out the jumble of words his eyes rested on Mrs Graham.

Elinor felt chagrined beyond bearing. She had meant to reveal her mother's presence in an atmosphere of cool sophistication. Now she was forced into introductions which he received in a manner half-mystified, half-amused. He was unexpectedly tanned by the sun, and his lithe beauty suddenly blotted out everything in Elinor's mind except the joy of his return. If only she possessed the right to throw her arms around his neck and savour a welcoming embrace! She felt the tears fill her eyes and hurried away to her room where she indulged in a weep before bathing her face, changing her gown and going downstairs.

Mr Brand grinned at her. 'Recovered?'

'Yes, thank you. I do not usually cry . . .'

' . . . unless it be absolutely necessary. Yes, I remember.'

She felt her temper slipping and recalled that they had parted in anger. Brown eyes and blue-grey locked, and the air was charged with words which cried for expression which was denied as Dominic ran into the room.

After dinner that night, when the tea had been finished and the others retired, Mr Brand and Elinor sat in easy chairs facing the open window. Elinor leaned back as the soft breezes ruffled her hair and cooled her hot forehead. The night was still, broken only by country noises beneath the darkening sky. Mr Brand looked peaceful, and abruptly Elinor resented his calm. She would stir up a turbulence to match her own.

'I was astonished when you left the manor in such a state to go on a trip.'

He turned his head sharply. 'Were you? And what sort of trip did I take?'

'One of pleasure! You went to enjoy yourself with your cronies.'

'I certainly enjoyed myself,' he replied laconically.

'I do not know how you could be so unkind as to abandon me to all the problems and without a word too. You managed to tell . . . others.'

'Others, Elinor?' His voice was soft.

'You left me a curt note,' she flashed.

'What others, Elinor?'

She tried to make her shrug nonchalant. 'The servants knew of your plans. So did Lady Sophia. She was quick to tell me.'

'Her ladyship came to tell you? You mean she gloated over you?'

'No!' Elinor wished she had not begun the conversation.

'What exactly are you saying?'

She took refuge in protest. 'You might have told *me*! I think it scandalous anyway that you should have gone off on a pleasure party in the midst of setting the manor to rights.'

There was a brief silence. Mr Brand's face was not clearly visible in the flickering candlelight. 'You seem always ready to imbue me with selfish motives.'

'I endeavour to be frank, sir.'

'A virtue indeed, though you would benefit by being in more command of your knowledge.'

'Do you deny that you left me with this . . . this incubus of a house, together with the responsibility of caring for its inmates? I did not even have Nancy to help!'

'I can scarcely be held responsible for her accident.'

His words were mildly said, but Elinor's raw nerves snapped. 'Go on, say it! Or for my mother and her party, who must be an embarrassment to you! The world will criticise you for sheltering her!'

'The world must do as it thinks best. I am judge of my actions.'

He rose and went to lean on the frame of the open window, staring into the garden. He looked weary, and Elinor was ashamed. He had been on the road for two days and not one word of reproach had he uttered about Mrs Graham.

He spoke evenly. 'Elinor, I did try to tell you of my plans, but could not seem to manage it. I have been to visit Mr Coke. I received an invitation from him.'

'I know.'

'But evidently you do not know that he has a famous reputation at home and abroad for lifting land cultivation and animal husbandry to extremely high standards. I have known him all my life and he has agreed to help me.'

'To help you?'

'You do not know me if you believe I would abandon anyone who depends on me.'

Elinor had a sick feeling in the pit of her stomach, yet a devil in her drove her on. 'My first impression of you was a drunken, gambling, dissolute . . .'

'And my first impression of you was of a young woman who had left the protection of a respectable home to persuade a bachelor to give her shelter even when she discovered that the man was young. Some might question *your* behaviour.'

She had asked for it, but his words stung unbearably. 'What a monstrous thing to say!'

He spoke as if he had not heard. 'I asked Mr Coke for advice. I missed the famous Holkham sheep-shearing, but he says that I should put healthy rams into my tenants' flocks. They will arrive later this year.'

'You have bought sheep!'

'I have also borrowed money. Mr Coke is always prepared to help landowners with good intent. I can repair the manor and the farms and cottages. I shall improve the soil. I *must* make the manor yield an income to repay the loan.'

She felt humble and her voice cracked. 'I . . . I am sorry. I should not have accused you.'

He too was contrite. 'I apologise, Elinor. I regret what I said.'

The rapport between them was sweet, and as Elinor took a hesitant step towards him he spoke again. 'There was no secrecy about my trip, but Lady Sophia learned of it when she asked me to view a property she may buy. She thinks she will spend part of the year in Gloucestershire, which she finds attractive.'

Her temper flared again. 'It is *you* she finds attractive!'

He stared at her, his face invisible in the shadows. He did not answer and she could only guess at his thoughts. If he had promised marriage to Lady Sophia she had the right to find him desirable. They would make a good match. Beauty and wealth allied to birth and property. Elinor felt bitter, while the ache to hold him close and speak of her love made her shake.

'I shall walk in the garden,' she gasped.

She fled to the shrubbery where she fought for control. A rustle of leaves made her peer in alarm. Perhaps Bastable was out here. She felt frightened and turned to run, colliding with a dark figure.

She shrieked and beat out with her fists as her elbows were gripped firmly and she was drawn close. She realised with shattering relief that she was held by her cousin.

'Oh, how you scared me,' she sobbed. 'I thought it was Bastable.'

The grip tightened to pain. 'Has he dared . . .?'

'He has not touched me, but his looks, his manner . . .'

He released her and she clung to his hands. His presence filled her world. He tried to pull away as she gasped, 'I missed you!' The words were so inadequate.

'Elinor . . . you make it difficult for me. It is impossible . . .'

He gave up and pulled her close until their bodies fused. She held up her face, her lips imploring the touch of his. Slowly he bent his head and she moaned. Then he thrust her from him. 'For God's sake! You are too damned tempting!'

He turned and strode to the house, flinging words over his shoulder at her. 'Come back in. If you and I are to remain here together you must learn that I am a man of flesh and blood who can be driven too far!'

'And what am I?' she cried.

He came back, grabbed her and almost dragged her to the manor. 'You are a girl of almost nineteen who requires—must have—a husband who can offer her what she wants.'

I know what I want, she screamed inwardly. *I want you! I love you!* Yet she could never tell him the truth. There was a vast gulf between his bodily passion and her true love.

In the house he handed her a lighted candle and escorted her to the stairs. She longed for some gentleness, but his face was set in masklike rigidity. She lay awake for a long time, her thoughts darting around her unhappy situation. Even if her cousin felt a stirring of love for her, he would destroy it. He

was a realist. He was also a man of will who had
turned his back on London life to take on all the
hard work and responsibility attached to his
ramshackle inheritance. He had to have money,
and Lady Sophia was anxious to give him hers. He
had, according to her, already sealed their bargain.

In the morning Elinor felt unrefreshed. Mr
Brand had been out early to invite his tenants to a
meeting that afternoon, and everyone was busy
washing all available tankards and glasses. Ale was
delivered from Stow-on-the-Wold and sugar-plums
and sweetmeats were set out for the children.

At two o'clock all was ready in the courtyard. For
half an hour no one appeared, then some of the
men trickled in. There were a couple of dozen who
drank the ale and listened without enthusiasm to
Mr Brand setting out his plans for them. Elinor saw
that their eyes went past her cousin to settle on
someone behind him. She walked suddenly
through the kitchen door to find Bastable leaning
on the wall in the shadows. He gave her a look of
dislike and mockery. By three o'clock the courtyard was empty and they gathered in the drawing-
room.

'Ungrateful wretches!' exclaimed Miss Tabitha.

Mr Brand shrugged. 'They have suffered abom-
inably. They are under-nourished. Their children
have died for want of food and medicine. The heart
is knocked out of them.'

He thanked Nancy for tea. 'They will listen
eventually. Meanwhile I shall pursue my enquiry
about the gipsy who died.'

'What a gruesome subject for so delightful a day!'
Lady Sophia strolled in.

Elinor felt twice as sticky from heat and anxiety as she saw that her ladyship looked fresh as a water-lily in a white gown with pale green ribbons and a straw hat. She accepted Mr Brand's compliments with easy grace and flirted with all her experienced coquetry.

She listened to the account of the disappointing meeting. 'Who can tell what transpires in the minds of the lower orders?' she said.

Mrs Graham said quietly, 'My servants have been invaluable to me.'

A frown creased her ladyship's white fore-head. 'Have you made any plans for your future, ma'am?'

Mrs Graham answered indirectly by turning to Mr Brand. 'I have been walking. There is a stone residence in the grounds. Would it be possible for Dominic and me to move there? I know that Dominic is a trial to . . . to some of the servants.'

Lady Sophia gave her a speculative look as Mr Brand answered, 'You are speaking of the Dower House. I see no reason why you should not occupy it, though it must be restored first. You are welcome to remain here meanwhile.'

Mrs Graham was relieved, but Lady Sophia looked displeased and Elinor wondered how he would fare with such an unkind woman. Perhaps he would tame her. Would her ladyship enjoy the process? Pictures which made her hot floated into her mind, and she hated Lady Sophia and she hated her cousin.

Late that evening Nurse came looking for Dominic.

Elinor was astonished. 'It is almost ten!'

'I know. Has anyone given permission for him to be out?'

No one had, but Mr Brand only smiled. 'He'll be fishing, I dare say. I remember playing such tricks myself. I suppose he'll have to be punished, but it makes one remember boyhood nostalgically.'

Nurse frowned. 'That's all very well, sir, but Master Dominic is wild. I don't think it's the first night he's been out.'

Mr Brand grinned. 'Maybe he's searching for your ghost, Elinor.'

Nurse said grimly. 'Like as not! That one would face the devil himself!' She marched out to return moments later to report that Dominic was now in his bed. 'He's pretending to be asleep, though from the poke I gave him he should have jumped up. Little varmint!'

As soon as Elinor was alone with her cousin she broke her indignant silence. 'Must you mock me by referring to *my* ghost?'

'No one else has seen it.'

'Your disbelief proves nothing!'

'I would not claim it did,' he responded easily. 'By the way, I gather that we could do with the old bakehouse ovens.'

'You had best consult Bastable, then,' she replied. 'And while you are about that, ask him why he stood half-concealed while you spoke to the villagers, and why they are so afraid of him.'

'He would not come out because he was sulking. I made him take his dog away.'

'That does not explain the fear.'

'More mysteries?'

'Yes! Add it to my non-existent ghost.'

He smiled. 'You need not be so cross. I am sure you heard something. Old houses have creaky beams. Or there could be mice . . .'

'. . . with iron-shod feet,' finished Elinor.

'Tomorrow,' said Mr Brand, firmly changing the subject, 'I shall give instructions for the bakehouse to be opened.'

'*Bon chance!*' cried Elinor as she swept him a mocking curtsey and retired to her room.

She wished she had not been so hasty. She was not tired and sat by the window reading a bound volume of *The Lady's Magazine* left by some long-departed woman. She was indignant to discover that the end of the serial was in the next volume and leaned back, closing her eyes. She awoke, stiff and cold, in a moonlit room, and she stretched and glanced out at the garden.

Two figures were making their way across the bright lawns of the manor where they disappeared through a side door. It was one o'clock. She reasoned with herself. One of them was Bastable, she felt sure. His master might not be pleased at his entertaining a friend so late, but he would prefer to be informed of it tomorrow, if at all. She should forget it and go to bed. But the instinct which insisted that something was wrong in the manor kept nagging at her and she decided to check her former room. Dominic was asleep there, so she would not be alone.

She slid through the bedchamber door, glancing at the four-poster with its drawn curtains where Dominic slept. Laying her ear to the wall she was left in no further doubt. The bangs and clangs rising up the chimney were not imagination. Something was being dragged across a surface, and now she could hear disembodied voices. She longed for Mr Brand's support, but if she went to him she could not be sure that the evidence would remain. What then? More humiliation?

She was amazed that the sounds did not disturb Dominic. Suddenly suspicious she pulled back the bed-curtains. The bed was empty. He had probably heard the sounds from the first and had been prowling at night ever since.

Elinor forced herself downstairs, across the hall trying not to see the empty eyes of the suits of armour, and put out her hand to open the door of the kitchen corridor.

In a terrifying repetition the dreadful white moaning shape floated out to hover over her head. But this time the outcome was different.

'I will catch him,' cried a voice. A small figure leapt from the shadows and tugged at the apparition, which gave a very human howl as Elinor's rescuer landed a kick. The ghost seemed to dissolve. Another small figure uncovered a candle lamp, which Elinor raised to reveal Tucker, who still clutched a broom over which he had hung a sheet. He was grasped by a gleeful Dominic while Jacky looked on.

'Your ghost, *mam'selle*,' grinned Dominic.

Elinor saw the old servant was by far the most frightened. His complexion had purpled and his eyes were staring. 'Let me be, young master,' he implored. 'It was only a . . . . a joke.'

'A joke!' exclaimed Elinor. 'You scared me half out of my wits. Why did you do it? And what are all those odd noises for?'

'Odd noises?' squeaked the butler. 'You're mistaken, miss.'

'No, I am not. You may as well tell the truth. When Mr Brand hears of this he will want to know.'

'I . . . I'll never do it again..I'm going.'

'You will remain where you are!'

The voice was controlled but it halted everyone.

'Cousin Christopher! You see, I was not fancying the ghost.'

Mr Brand came into the small pool of light. He had dressed quickly in boots and breeches, and his shirt was half buttoned. Elinor dragged her eyes from him. He looked even more attractive.

'I thought Joe was playing pranks,' admitted Mr Brand. 'I intended to question him. Release Tucker, Dominic.' The old man rubbed his wrist and Mr Brand said, 'We shall go to the kitchen.'

Tucker slumped hopelessly and they followed Mr Brand. The kitchen was empty, and Tucker suddenly coughed very loudly and artificially, but was not quick enough to smother a chink of metal which came from the direction of the large cupboard.

Mr Brand spoke softly. 'It is time I investigated.'

Dominic said in excited whispers, 'I have been trying to track down the noises ever since I slept in that room. They always stopped by the time I got here. Twice that funny old man has jumped out on me with his sheet. I ran away the first time!'

Elinor wondered why the gipsy boy was silent, and saw that he had slipped out. She looked through the swinging outer door and caught sight of a small figure hurried along by a girl whose black hair reached her waist. Jacky's sister would take good care of him.

Mr Brand had put his hands on one side of the cupboard and gave a gentle push. He grinned. 'Did you see it move? I am not so strong as it seems. It is on oiled runners, is it not, Tucker?'

The butler was incapable of speech or opposition, and when he was told to stand to one side of the cupboard he obeyed. 'Now, Elinor, you and Dominic join Tucker, and whatever happens do not get in my line of fire.

Elinor stared at the deadly-looking small pistol produced by her cousin, as Dominic argued, 'I want to join the fun.'

'Obey me,' ordered Mr Brand dispassionately, 'or I shall give you the thrashing for which you have been asking.'

'You would, too,' Dominic said admiringly, and ranged himself beside Elinor.

Mr Brand placed the candle on the table and stood in shadow. 'Now, push,' he said to Tucker.

The butler leaned and the huge cupboard moved to reveal a dark open doorway.

'Come out slowly and carefully,' called Mr Brand.

There was no sound and Tucker quavered, 'See, there's nothing there.'

'Nothing!' Dominic ran forward to peer in the aperture and two men sprang out, colliding with the boy and knocking him down. One took a kick at the table and the candle fell and went out.

Elinor heard her cousin curse as the men raced for the kitchen door and fled into the night.

'You young idiot,' she said, as she hauled Dominic to his feet. 'Are you hurt?'

'No! I am so sorry,' he wailed.

Mr Brand stared into the garden. 'I could not shoot,' he said. 'I might have hit someone innocent. I recognised Bastable, and I think the other man was a gipsy.' He lifted the candle. 'Now we shall see what this is all about. No, Dominic, you will allow me to go first.'

He edged his way into the old bakehouse and Elinor held her breath. What if someone else lurked inside?

His voice came muffled. 'You may enter.'

Elinor and Dominic almost jammed in the door in their haste and looked in amazement at a heap of battered saucepans.

'Open the oven doors,' ordered Mr Brand.

Dominic obeyed. 'Look! Silver! Dishes, and cups and candle holders. I knew that bad servant was one of the robbers! I wish I had caught him! I would give the reward to Tante Marianne!'

They returned to the kitchen and Tucker resignedly pushed the cupboard back and inserted the wedges which kept it stable. Dominic was ordered to go to bed and sloped off, still subdued.

Tucker's teeth were chattering as he stared at Mr Brand. 'What you going to do, sir? Are you going to tell on us? I didn't want any part of it, but Bastable made me. Everyone's afraid of him.'

'It wasn't only robbery, was it, Tucker?'

The butler's eyes protruded in terror. 'No, sir. How did you find out?'

'I saw the braziers and the ladles, the charcoal and moulds. They were in a corner of the bakehouse.'

Tucker babbled: 'It started when Bastable came back from London. He'd learned how to make copper coins. It was all right at first. The gipsies passed them at the fairs and no one takes no notice of bad copper. But then he got greedy. He wasn't content with coins made from old pans. He stole folks' silver and said we was to dip the coins. That's a capital offence, sir.'

Elinor was shocked. 'You mean you could be hanged?'

'Or transported, miss, and who ever comes back from transportation?' He tugged at his neckcloth as if he felt a hangman's rope.

'How many people know about it?' asked Mr Brand.

'Only me and my wife, sir, and Bastable, of course, and the gipsies. Folk know who done the robberies, but they kept their eyes and ears shut. But we've all been scared out of out wits since the gipsy lad was killed.'

'Was that Bastable?' Mr Brand sounded grim.

'No one knows for certain, though it's my belief Luther died because he wouldn't handle silver counterfeit coins. He didn't want terrible trouble brought on his tribe. Luther was the clever one at making moulds. Since he died Bastable's been doing it, and the coins are poor. I've been living in dread that we'd get caught. It's a relief it's over!'

'I see.' Mr Brand regarded the old man with a tinge of pity. 'Must I lock you up, or will you stay here?'

Tucker's shoulders sagged. 'Me and my old woman got nowhere else.'

He dragged his feet as he left and Elinor asked, 'Will anyone need to be told about him?'

Mr Brand replied thoughtfully, 'Perhaps not. He

and his wife may not be the only servants to be implicated in the robberies. Many are related to the villagers, and there has been great intimidation. If this is the end of the matter I would prefer not to ruin any more lives.' He looked around. 'Where is Jacky?'

'He ran off.' Elinor said nothing of Zenobia, whom she pitied.

Mr Brand looked into her face. 'You have had too many shocks, and I have not helped you. Do you forgive me?'

Elinor could scarcely articulate. Forgive him! Nothing had matched the turmoil of her love for him. She managed a few strangled words. Then the night was ripped apart by screams which held them transfixed. Mr Brand raced for the door.

'Stay in, Elinor! Try to pacify the others.'

She ran to watch him until his figure disappeared into the darkness of the trees.

CHAPTER
TEN

ELINOR was fully engaged in calming the fears of an awakened household. 'It is someone playing foolish pranks,' she insisted. 'Mr Brand has gone to see.'

Dominic did not appear, and when she checked she found he had left the house. She finished soothing her mother, managing to conceal the boy's absence and wandered into the library, where she sank into a chair, wondering what had happened to her cousin. Bastable was evil and was somewhere outside.

In spite of her anxiety she fell into an uneasy doze and when a touch brushed her cheek she leapt in alarm. Mr Brand was bending over her. Her skin tingled where his fingers had touched her.

'What happened? I have been so worried!'

'You will be shocked, my dear. Bastable is dead. It was Betsy who screamed.'

'Did she kill him?'

'No! If she had she would have shown clear signs. The murder was brutal, and she loved him in spite of his character. She is distraught.'

Mr Brand pulled back the shabby velvet curtains and opened the long window to admit dawn air and light. 'I brought villagers to tend the body and care for Betsy, then I rode to Sir Henry. I am afraid his chief suspect is Zenobia.'

'Oh, no! I won't believe it!'

Then she stopped, remembering the girl's presence in the garden. 'Why her?'

'She is known to have vowed vengeance on whoever killed her man.'

'But no one knows who did that! *Was* it Bastable?'

Mr Brand shrugged. 'I don't think anyone is sure. Zenobia is wanted so that she may be questioned. We went to the encampment and found the gipsies packing to leave. They now have a guard on them.'

When Mr Brand learned that Dominic was out he looked irritated, then sat down wearily. 'He can probably look after himself better than most. Is there any food? I am famished.'

In the kitchen he downed bread and butter with peach preserve, and Elinor made sure the coffee was hot and strong. She watched him, dreaming of living their lives in such sweet intimacy, until he jerked her back to reality.

'Your hauntings were real, after all. The bakehouse is directly below the bedchamber.'

Resentful of any intrusion into her pleasant imaginings, Elinor retorted, 'It is a pity you did not listen to me.'

His brows rose. 'You can scarcely blame me! Ever since we met you have been proving how wilful you are. I thought you determined to have your own way in this. There was no evidence presented to *me*.'

Their rapport was shattered and Elinor said, 'Why did not the coiners leave the manor when we came?'

'Where could they go? Such activities are very

difficult to hide.' He finished his coffee. 'Excellent! What a pity you are determined to be a rich man's wife. Your culinary skill will be wasted.'

He left to change his clothes and Elinor put the dishes in the sink, keeping a tight guard on herself so that she did not smash them in her frustrated fury. But when her cousin left again her anger died and she ached to have the right to hold him close and beg him to be careful for her sake.

The day dragged by. Elinor wondered often what was happening and whether or not Dominic was with the searchers. Mrs Graham seemed complacently sure that he was, but at the dinner hour Nurse said, looking grim, 'Master Dominic is missing.'

Elinor kept calm. 'I am sure he is with the men.'

'No, he isn't. Tucker's been to the village and he said all the men had met for discussion, and Dominic hadn't been seen.'

Mrs Graham went pale and could eat almost nothing, retiring at once to her room, clinging to an assertion that the boy must be playing pranks.

Elinor followed her. Her mother was seated near the window, her hands clenched. 'Dominic is wilful—and daring,' she said distractedly, 'exactly like his father.' She stopped, staring at Elinor with an expression which sent her cold.

'I thought he was a waif you had found, ma'am. Did you know his father well?'

'Oh, very well indeed.' Tears sprang to her eyes 'Oh, Elinor, I am so anxious! Dominic is my son!'

'Your son! My half-brother?'

'I had meant to keep it secret . . .'

'Where is his father?'

'He could not marry me, he already had a wife. But I did love him, Elinor, and he loved me.'

Elinor looked at Mrs Graham. If the barriers between herself and Christopher Brand had not already been insurmountable, this new one must keep them apart. What gentleman would marry a girl whose own mother acknowledged a base-born child?

'Others have been worse than I,' sobbed Mrs Graham. 'Beauty was my only asset. I had to use it.'

'Have there been others?'

'A few! But I always cared for them, Elinor. I am not so bad!'

For a brief moment Elinor felt sick with rage at a mother who could abandon her daughter then return to poison her life. But her anger died. Her mother was foolish, vain and immoral, but she needed protection. Perhaps it was this realisation that had kept her father so forgiving. And Dominic was guiltless.

Downstairs she learned that a gipsy woman was enquiring for her at the kitchen door. She was disappointed to find a stranger.

'Have you seen Jacky? Mazel sent me to ask.'

Elinor shook her head. 'But Dominic is also missing! Perhaps the boys are together. Where is Zenobia?'

The woman threw her a look of distrust. 'She be where the gorgios won't find her.'

Elinor said urgently. 'Only tell me she is safe. I wish her well.'

'Safe, is it? I reckon so, though wed to Draco 'tis not likely she'll be happy.'

'But she hates him!'

The woman hissed, 'I've said too much. I'll be beaten . . .'

Mr Brand returned at ten o'clock. He poured a glass of brandy and downed it. When Elinor told him of the gipsy woman's visit he said, 'The boys could be together, I suppose. I saw Mazel, and she is as anxious as we are. She refused to discuss Zenobia.'

'She is with Draco. They are to be married.'

'Is that so?' He poured a smaller brandy and held the glass in his palms, twisting it gently. 'I see you do not reprimand me for over-indulgence.'

'Will you always remember everything I said?'

He smiled and sank into a chair. 'I like to recall many things about you, my dear.'

Colour flared in her face. 'How can you be so calm? There is so much trouble and worry.'

'I am doing everything I can to help, but all I know for certain is that the manor has been used for an illegal purpose. I am glad the miscreants have fled and I deplore murder, even of such a rogue as Bastable. I pray the boys are off on some adventurous game of their own.'

'What of Zenobia? Cannot you pity a girl forced into a horrible marriage?'

'Who is forcing her? She doesn't have to marry him, even if he is helping her to escape.' At Elinor's furious exclamation he said, 'You are allowing sentiment to rule reason. A typical feminine fault!'

She refused to see the laughter in his eyes. 'Indeed, sir! And it is typical of an insensitive male to imagine that Zenobia would wed a man unless she loved him truly. What an abhorrent notion!'

She caught her breath as his humour turned to

mockery. She waited for his reply in quivering nervousness.

He said lazily, 'You intend to marry someone who can support you in a way of life you desire. There was no mention of love when we met.'

She felt she would burst with protest. She longed to explain how her attitude had altered, but then she might reveal her love for him. And he did not care for her! She could not endure such debasement. She knew that his caresses had been a casual amusement to him.

He had leaned back and closed his eyes and was asleep. Lines of weariness traced their pattern on his face and Elinor's tumult died. She burned to touch his face with her lips. To arouse him to a display of passion which would sweep them into ecstasy. She felt wanton and shameful. She was envious of every woman he had ever embraced, and loathed Lady Sophia, who held him in her spoiled hands.

One hour drifted into another, and she crept to the window and stared into the garden. Something moved in the shadows and her heart jumped. Zenobia stepped into a patch of moonlight which gleamed on her black hair. Elinor leaned out and called softly and slowly the girl came to her.

'Zenobia, they said you were with Draco! Is he here?' Zenobia glanced around nervously.

'That brute! I've left him!'

'I knew it could not be true that you were to marry him.'

Both girls started as Mr Brand spoke from behind Elinor. 'Come into the house, Zenobia. We must talk.'

The gipsy girl hesitated, then moved forward and stepped through into the library. 'I must trust someone,' she muttered. She accepted a chair and continued wearily, 'I had to come here. I want everyone to know the truth.'

'You did not kill anyone, did you?' begged Elinor, disregarding her cousin's frown.

'Not I! But I have behaved foolishly. I put my poor little brother in danger by sending him to watch Bastable. I thought he murdered my Luther.'

'Is Dominic with Jacky now?' asked Mr Brand sharply.

Zenobia looked at him with wide dark eyes. 'Not that I know of. But I can only guess at where my brother be.' She shrugged. 'I do not know.' She sipped the wine and colour stole into her face. 'Jacky's most likely with Mazel by now. I'll tell you what happened from the start. We gipsies knew of the coining, but only Draco wanted to follow Bastable when he decided to silver the coins. That's a capital offence, sir, as you know. When my Luther refused to help he was killed. I know now that Draco did it.'

'I was told you were going to marry him!' cried Elinor.

Zenobia tossed her head angrily. 'We believed him when he said he had destroyed Bastable after he'd learned that he was the one who killed Luther. Mazel said it was my duty to reward him for his just vengeance by going away with him and wedding him.'

'What brought you back?' asked Mr Brand.

'The truth! My brother followed us. Poor little fellow—he was terrified. He waited till Draco slept, then crept to me. He explained how he'd seen Luther's murder, and that Draco was more guilty than Bastable. The two men caught Jacky as he tried to slip away and told him that if he betrayed them the *mulos* would get him.'

'*Mulos*!' exclaimed Elinor.

Zenobia's eyes looked fearful. 'They be the spirits of the dead. Then even said that our parents be *mulos* now and would haunt him. They frightened my poor brother of his own mother and father! But Jacky couldn't let me marry with a man who killed my true love. Draco woke and heard us talking. He tried to catch Jacky. I hit Draco with a stick and he fell down. Then Jacky and I came back to the camp. I couldn't get in because of the guards, but Jacky ran ahead to tell Mazel what had happened. I don't know where he be now.'

'But I do!'

The softly menacing voice spun them to face the window. Draco stepped through and stood looking at them, an ugly sneer on his face, made more dark by a heavy bruise on his forehead. He touched the mark with his fingertips, not taking his eyes from Zenobia. 'So! My woman runs to the gorgios. Get your shawl and come with me!'

'Murderer! I would die first!'

'But will you let Jacky die? Or the little master?'

Elinor cried out in horror, but her cousin kept his voice level. 'Have you harmed the boys?'

'Not *yet*! They be my price.'

'Is it ransom you want?' Mr Brand demanded curtly.

'Aye, you might say so—my price be freedom. I've no mind to lose my life for killing a gorgio.'

'What about Luther?' cried Zenobia. 'He was your own blood brother!'

'That was an accident!' snarled the gipsy.

'Where are the boys?' demanded Elinor.

Draco glared at her from bloodshot eyes. 'That's for you to know when I get what I'm after.'

'Which is?' asked Mr Brand.

'Horses for me and Zenobia and gold to pay our way.'

'Never mind getting a mount for me,' grated Zenobia. 'I'll not go with him again.'

Draco's eyes narrowed. 'I came back for you. I want you! I'll do no bargaining unless you come with me.'

There was a brief silence into which Zenobia's words dropped like slivers of glass. 'Best not take me, Draco, 'cause if you do you'll never dare turn your back on me, or sleep, unless you lock your door. My Luther ain't avenged yet.'

Elinor shivered as she watched Draco's face grow darker with bitter rage. He spoke in low tones. 'A horse for me! And gold—as much as you've got.'

'Where are the boys?'

'I'll send back word.'

Mr Brand looked at the gipsy contemptuously. 'That is not enough.'

Draco stepped close to Mr Brand, his fist clenched, and Elinor remembered that this man had killed twice. But her cousin kept his eyes fixed on Draco, who saw that he would not—could not—compromise.

'If I tell you, how do I know you'll let me go?'

'Don't judge him by your own evil ways,' spat out Zenobia.

Mr Brand said, 'You will have to take my word, Draco. Once I am satisfied that the boys are safe I will give you your ransom and twelve hours' start. I promise no more.'

Draco's rage was a tangible evil which filled the room and he emitted a stream of Romany which made Zenobia's lip curl. At last he said, 'I don't have to give in to you, gorgio! I could go the way I came and you'd never find them.'

Zenobia sprang past Mr Brand's restraining hand and confronted the gipsy, her black eyes snapping. 'Leave on foot—if you dare! Without that start you'll never cross the next county! Your brothers would make sure you never saw another sunset!'

Terror flickered in Draco's eyes. 'I'll tell you where they be. Let's be quick.'

'Not before we have witnesses to the fact that Zenobia is innocent of any murders,' said Mr Brand.

All the gipsy's suspicions returned. 'It be a trick!'

No one answered him and he muttered, 'Who'll watch me make my mark?'

'Miss Graham and a trusted member of my household,' answered Mr Brand.

They waited as birds sang in the garden to announce the dawn. Finally Draco nodded.

Mr Brand turned to Elinor. 'Bring Nurse here.'

CHAPTER
ELEVEN

ZENOBIA and Elinor waited alone in the library.
Nurse had been fetched and, after Elinor had asked
for her help, had signed the paper. She had looked
curiously at the gipsies, but promised to keep silent
about them. At the door she paused. 'Will Master
Dominic be brought back safe?'

Mr Brand had reassured her and the old woman
had left. Now Elinor tried to keep her thoughts
from her cousin, riding through the darkness with a
man who was merciless and desperate. Zenobia sat
in a half-crouch on a sofa, her arms hugged about
her body, a shiver passing over her sometimes. It
seemed an eternity before Zenobia's eyes lit up and
she raised her head.

'I hear hoofbeats!'

Elinor could hear them now, and both girls
sprang to their feet and waited. The door opened
and Mr Brand entered.

'The boys are safe, thank God. I sent Jacky
straight to the camp, Zenobia. Your brother is wise
for his years. I told him how things are, and he will
remain silent about Draco until you give him leave
to speak. I hope that Mazel understands.'

Zenobia gave a little shrug. 'She will. It is of no
consequence, anyhow. My Luther will be avenged,

and Draco knows it. His return for me was not born of love. He decided to possess me before his death, which will come soon.'

She sounded almost dispassionate and suddenly Elinor wanted to be free of the presence of the girl and the dark pictures she conjured. 'Where can she hide?' she asked Mr Brand.

Zenobia's weary eyes seemed to bore into Elinor's brain and wrest every secret from it. 'You are not made for my kind of life, gorgio woman, yet the fires of your body are like mine. I hope you get the man you want.'

Mr Brand threw an enigmatic glance at Elinor before saying, 'The old bakehouse is locked and I hold the key. It is dark and without comfort, but would be a perfect refuge. It is only for a day.'

Zenobia's face shadowed. 'I shall be shut between four walls! That was what my Luther feared most. It was why he wouldn't make the moulds for the silver coins, and why he died.' She moved to the door. 'I shall keep my vow for twelve hours.'

Elinor went first to the kitchen where she was greeted by a rapturous Dominic, and helped him to carry a large quantity of food to a small parlour where he continued his dedicated mastication.

She and her cousin helped Zenobia into the old bakehouse, giving her cushions, blankets, food and drink, candles and flints. The door was locked and the huge cupboard rolled into place and wedged fast.

After Elinor had tidied away any trace of the gipsy girl's presence she asked, 'Why did Draco kill Bastable?'

'I asked him that. It was for the same greed which

was the cause of the first murder. Much of the profit from the coining is still to come from the gipsies, who are passing coins at fairs all over the country, and the men had no intention of abandoning their crimes. Bastable demanded a larger share of the proceeds. When Draco refused him, he threatened to tell the gipsies that Draco was the principal killer of Luther—he wrote his own death warrant. Within minutes he lay dead.'

'Does life mean nothing to them?'

'They are not all so violent,' said Mr Brand, 'but honour means everything to them. I must respect them for that, at least.'

'Honour!' Elinor's voice was raspingly angry. 'I suppose they are no different from society men who fight duels and risk life and health for almost nothing!'

'I have not fought a duel,' protested Mr Brand.

'I am sure you would if you felt it necessary!' snapped Elinor. The sudden release from tension gave her a need to lash about her with words. Her cousin seemed to understand, for he merely drew the coffee pot from the kitchen fire he had poked into flame and poured two cups.

Elinor saw that when he held the pot he winced, and she jeered, 'Don't you know enough not to burn your hands?'

He gave her a look in which humour and reproach mingled. 'I hope I do. They got damaged by some exceedingly sharp brambles.'

Elinor held his hands between her own. 'Oh, what dreadful scratches! You will get poisoned!'

'Nonsense!'

She fetched a bowl and warm water and cloths

and bathed his wounds carefully as he watched her, still with the ironical gleam in his eyes. She patted his hands dry, resisting a powerful impulse to kiss them, and he drank his coffee.

'What happened?' she asked.

'Dominic and Jacky were in a small underground cavern. Draco had rolled an enormous boulder over the entrance which was concealed by the brambles. He moved the stone without help—he must be far stronger than he looks.'

Elinor shuddered. 'Horrible man! And he carries a knife! What chance would you have stood with him?'

'I had a gun! I am not such a fool—or a weakling,' protested Mr Brand.

Elinor opened her mouth to deny she believed him anything but perfect, but she was saved from such a revealing disclosure by Dominic who wandered into the kitchen, still chewing. He peered at the scene and saw the deep scratches. 'You should have worn gloves.'

Elinor was indignant. 'Is that all you can say?'

'I am very glad that Mr Brand saved us,' declared Dominic.

Elinor fetched more water and washed the boy's bruises as he squirmed and protested.

'Keep still, you little fiend,' she ordered. 'If you had not run from the manor you would not have suffered.'

'You are right!' Dominic sounded convinced. 'I was bad, that I know, but I had a very great curiosity about the screams. It was that nasty Betsy! She was squealing like a stuck pig over Bastable. He was dead. I think she really liked him. How I do not know! I do not, even if he is dead!'

He turned to Mr Brand. 'Why must one like people when they are dead?' He did not await an answer. 'I was running back to the manor when I bumped into Draco. He is very vile! He was covered in blood. He grabbed me, and when I kicked and bit him he hit me and I went unconscious. When I woke up I was in that little hole and Jacky was dropping tears on me because he thought I was dead. We had a little candle, but it burnt out.'

Elinor shivered. 'Horrible! How you must have suffered!'

'We did,' agreed Dominic, 'though I told Jacky that Mr Brand would find us. I know he is clever.'

Mr Brand expressed his gratification at such trust, and then Elinor sent Dominic to Nurse. 'Wake her gently,' she cautioned. 'Get her to change your clothes before you visit your . . . Tante Marianne.'

She put the bowls and cloths away, flushing as she realised how nearly she had betrayed her new knowledge about Dominic. When she turned her cousin was watching her compassionately.

'You have guessed that Dominic is your mamma's own child?'

Her flush deepened. 'How long have you known?'

'Almost from the beginning. There is a likeness in their expressions. Besides, she gives herself away—she would not make a diplomat.'

Elinor felt sick as the full realisation of this added barrier swamped her. 'It is easy to criticise. She has paid for her first mistake. Once she had run from my father she could never regain her position in society. Unlike a man! A man can do anything and he is forgiven!'

Mr Brand's brows drew together. 'I was not criticising. I do not make the rules, and I refuse to quarrel with you on such an issue. I like Mrs Graham and I have offered her a home.'

'What about Lady Sophia?' Elinor wished the words unsaid immediately.

He looked amazed. 'I do not have to consult her before giving someone a tenancy!'

Elinor walked out of the kitchen. If she stayed she would say things about her ladyship which must be kept inside her. She was her cousin's choice and Elinor must grow accustomed to it. But she did not have to like it, or pretend that she did. And she need not stay to witness their union. She stood by her open window, holding her hands to her burning face, allowing the fragrant morning breeze to waft through her hair. She looked in her mirror and groaned. What a sight! Face fiery red, and hair tangled and unbrushed. There were even smuts on her nose from the kitchen hob.

She tidied herself before Nancy entered with tea and bread and butter. Elinor parried her excited questions and comments and asked for plenty of hot water. Then she lay in her bath before the fire, breathing in the scented steam as if it were a cleansing incense. Afterwards she towelled herself hard, and put on a lilac sprigged muslin gown with matching knots of satin. She brushed her hair until it shone and tied it with a lilac ribbon.

She avoided the others and wandered into the garden. Joe was scything the grass and the clean, fresh smell wafted over her as he looked up with his foolish smile. She walked to the edge of the woodland. All her senses were vibrantly alive and she was conscious of every sound, every scent, every breath of air. She looked back at the manor. It was beginning to show improvement. It looked lived in—cared for. It looked like home. The idea took her by surprise and it frightened her, for the manor could never be her home.

A feeling of desolation swept over her and her regret at the ending of the adventure was bitter. She would have kept the danger, the worry, the uncertainty, for a further chance of remaining near her cousin's side. Christopher! She whispered aloud the name which her heart had used for a long time.

Miss Tabitha came out of the manor door and descended the steps, carrying a basket. Elinor stepped back quickly into the shadows of the trees, then turned and began to hurry along the first path she reached. It had recently been cleared and she moved fast, her need for solitude driving her on.

Rounding a bend she found herself facing the Dower House. The front door sagged on its hinges and the whole place exuded a sense of ruin. It epitomised Elinor's despair at the collapse of her dreams. When she remembered how blithely she had set off from Miss Brown's Academy, how arrogantly sure she had been in her cousin's London house, she went hot with embarrassment and regret. No wonder Christopher rejected her! A young woman who demanded succour of a bachelor cousin could not be thought to possess the proper feeling necessary in a wife.

She wandered up the mossy path to the house and stepped inside. The odorous smell of damp wood made her gulp. It would take a great amount of money to make the place habitable. The loan which Christopher had would not last forever, and was not intended to effect such repairs. His people needed all the help he could give them. *He* needed Lady Sophia and her wealth. Elinor was convinced that her ladyship would consider it a matter of urgency to restore the Dower House before she did anything else. She would never countenance Mrs Graham and Dominic beneath her roof.

She wandered through the rooms, then walked upstairs and peeped into the bedchambers. She saw that it could be turned into a pleasant haven and hoped that her mother would find here the peace she craved. Suddenly overwhelmed by gratitude towards a man who would not be blamed if he spurned his cousin and her child, Elinor walked to the head of the stairway. She had not expressed appreciation of Christopher's action, and she would find him and make good her omission. She owed him that much.

She had paused a moment and realised that in her absorption she had not realised that there was someone in the house. Her heart jumped before she reminded herself that the dangers of the past weeks were over. She would stay quite still and whoever was downstairs might go away. It could be a poacher, she thought, or a workman looking round.

'Who is there?'

The question came sharply up the stairs and she clung to the landing rail as she identified the newcomer as her Cousin Christopher.

A few moments ago she had been anxious to find

him. Now, perversely, she was equally anxious to remain hidden from him. A sudden aching vulnerability made her raw.

'I know someone is upstairs!' His voice was calm and decisive. 'I promise you I shall not be angry, whoever you are. Please come down. The floors are quite rotten in places, and no one should be here until they have been repaired.'

Elinor wished passionately that she had moved naturally when first he spoke. Now she had delayed revealing herself until he had begun to cajole, and she was feeling disinclined to meet him under the increasingly humiliating circumstances.

He put a step on the bottom stair. He was coming up! Trying to seem nonchalant, she moved to the top of the stairs. Christopher, half hidden in the shadows thrown by the encroaching bushes and trees, peered upwards as she began the descent, then his eyes widened with astonishment.

'Elinor! Is that you? Why didn't you answer me?'

She finished walking down the stairs and stood close to him. 'May I pass?' Her voice was distant and cool.

Christopher stepped down and back. 'Certainly! If you had wanted to inspect your mother's new home I would have brought you myself. You should not be risking yourself on these rotting boards.'

Elinor did her best to make her shrug casual. 'I have come to no harm.'

Christopher's voice contained suppressed annoyance. 'Your answer to everything, is it not? Do you intend to pursue the rest of your life taking chances which could bring you danger?'

'I have no idea what you mean!'

'Have you not? You have no intention of remaining safely with your relatives until you can be chaperoned into society! You will go off on some other harebrained scheme, only this time you may not meet with the forbearance I have shown. Well, don't come running to me with your tears when you have been hurt!'

'You are the last person to whom I would apply, sir.'

'Oh, I am sure of that! And of course, you never cry, do you?'

Elinor turned her back on him, gazing out of a window on to a tangle of roots and weeds. She hung on to her self-control, knowing that if once she let go she would prove she could weep with abandon. When she felt calmer she turned. If she walked out now she could pass him and reach the door and hurry into the woods where she could hide her misery from him. She made the mistake of casting one anguished glance at him, and was seized with a longing so intense that she wondered if it was visible in a miasmic shroud. Surely it could not be possible to hurt so much without revealing something?

In her haste to escape she did not take the care the floor needed. She stepped on to a wet patch of wood she had previously avoided and her foot slipped. In an effort to regain her balance she flung out her arms, teetered and fell, her foot going through the rotten boards. A sharp pain in her ankle made her cry out and Christopher was on his knees, his hands on her foot, his voice gently soothing.

She gasped as he broke the diseased wood to

release her, and he slid his arm about her shoulders. 'Lean on me, Elinor.'

Half-hopping, she reached an abandoned chair which emitted a cloud of dust as she sank into it. 'Now I shall have to wash my gown,' she said irrelevantly, a sob in her voice. He rightly ignored the remark and knelt on the dirty boards, probing her ankle with knowing fingers.

'One might suppose you to have learned doctoring!' Why could she not keep the ridicule from her voice? His behaviour did not warrant it.

'A man with limited means gets accustomed to examining his dogs and horses,' was his reply, delivered in cold, dispassionate tones.

Elinor gasped. Did he regard her with no more feeling than he would a prized animal? Less, she supposed. Of what use could she be to him?

Any reply she might have made was lost in a sharp intake of breath as jagged pain in her ankle rendered her speechless.

'There! That's better!'

'I am glad you think so! What did you do?'

'I removed this!' Christopher held up a large sliver of wood. 'You have quite a nasty wound. We had best get you back to bathe and bandage it.'

'You need not bother,' she said distantly. 'I came out to . . . to walk alone, and I do not intend my outing to be spoilt by . . .'

Her voice trailed off as her cousin rose and stood glaring down at her. 'Wilful! It is a great pity that no one took you in hand years ago.'

Elinor also rose, stifling a small cry as she put her foot to the floor. 'My upbringing was everything I desired, thank you. Now I shall continue my walk.'

'You will go back to the house and allow someone to bathe you!'

'I shall do no such thing!'

For a moment they stared angrily into each
other's eyes. Elinor's heart was thumping so violently she knew she was shaking, but she made an
attempt to push past him.

An instant came and went when she thought he
would try to restrain her physically, and she could
not tell whether she was more relieved or disappointed as he allowed her to go.

Her turbulent emotions kept her moving for a
short way along a path between trees until the pain
in her ankle became persistently throbbing, and she
stopped. She leaned on the wide bole of a beech, all
the rebellion dying in her. A sound of trickling
water lifted her head. She hobbled in the direction
of the water and came upon a tiny stream which
tumbled its way over pebbles and sand. Her ankle
felt as if it was on fire, and she sank on to a warm
patch of grass where sunlight broke through. She
slipped off her kid shoe and slid her stockinged foot
into the water; the cool movement on the wound
was a delight and she continued to sit, adding her
other foot to be caressed by the stream.

As she sighed and got up, using a handful of dried
grass to wipe her feet before slipping her shoes back
on, she heard Christopher's voice a few feet away.

'Now perhaps you will admit your weakness and
allow me to assist you back to the manor.'

She blushed, wondering how long he had been
watching her. 'To spy upon a lady is scarcely the
action of a gentleman,' she flashed.

'You have already granted me so many imperfections that one more can make no difference,' he answered, holding out an arm covered in rough country cloth.

She placed her fingertips upon it, attempting to walk without taking the least advantage of his strength. She managed it for a few paces until the numbing effect obtained by the water wore off, then the pain made her bite her lips and she stumbled.

Instantly his arm was round her. He held her close and she felt the heat of his body. Her self-control splintered into a million fragments. She gave a tiny moan and put her head on his shoulder, her hat falling back and hanging by the strings.

'My God!' he said, between his teeth. 'It isn't to be borne. Elinor . . .'

She felt his mouth on her hair. His hands turned her urgently and his eyes blazed into hers. Their mouths fused in a kiss of naked desire, then she pushed against him violently. 'No! How dare you!'

'I dare,' he said, 'I dare, Elinor.'

Again he pulled her close and as his lips covered hers she surrendered to long moments of ecstasy before once more dragging herself away. She kept her head turned as she mumbled, 'You are base, sir!'

He stiffened with the shock of her rejection. Then he said softly, 'Elinor, you blow hot and cold. Is this how you amuse yourself? Does it give you pleasure to promise me so much with your embrace, then deny me?'

'Does it give you pleasure, sir, to toy with a woman in such a manner when you are betrothed to another?'

'I am *what*?'

His fury seemed genuine and she was puzzled. 'You are to wed Lady Sophia!'

'Have I told you that?'

Rage exploded within her. 'No! You have told me nothing. You seek to make love to me illicitly, but her ladyship has not kept your betrothal a secret. She . . .'

'My *what*?' This time there could be no mistaking his anger. 'Lady Sophia informed you that we are engaged to be married? My God! No wonder your behaviour is so erratic!'

'I am not nearly so erratic as you! To be promised to one woman while attempting to seduce another . . .'

She was stopped by his harsh laughter. 'Is there nothing with which you do not accuse me? I am surprised you did not set down murder to my other sins!'

Elinor stared at him. 'You are not going to marry Lady Sophia?'

'Give me credit for some sense, even if you think my honour so small a thing!'

'Say it! Tell me it is not true!'

'Did she say it was?'

Elinor nodded and Christopher touched her cheek with a gentle finger. 'Poor girl! No wonder you have been so bewildered by me. Yet you kissed me. Not once, but several times. And you have allowed me to believe . . .'

'Be quiet,' she begged.

'. . . to believe that you want to hold me as much as I do you. You permitted this, even believing that I was betrothed to someone else.'

'I suppose you have thought me wanton,' she gasped.

'Wanton? Oh, no! Impetuous—reckless even at times . . .'

His hands were behind her back, pulling her inexorably to him. 'Now I have only the sweetest thoughts of you, my love. Say the words I feared I'd never hear. Tell me you love me.'

'I love you,' she said on a sob. 'I love you so much.'

'Elinor, I adore you. I never thought it possible to care for a woman as much as I do for you.'

Their kiss was as gentle and tender as if it were their first, then it deepened into the yearning hunger which consumed them. They gazed at one another and tasted again the promise of their joy to come. At last Christopher said, 'We must return to the house, my darling. We shall waste no time in getting married, I promise you.'

Elinor leaned on him and they strolled along the woodland path. Her ankle scarcely hurt at all, or did she not notice it.

He looked down at her. 'Would you have gone away without revealing how much you love me if I had not followed you today?'

'Perhaps.' She shuddered. 'How terrible to think we might have missed our happiness.'

'Terrible!' he agreed.

They stopped to examine for a moment a decaying log busy with insects, using the opportunity for another satisfying embrace.

Christopher asked, 'How could you think I would tie myself to a female like Lady Sophia?'

Elinor grinned and said with a return of asperity,

'Men often marry dreadful women, especially when they are rich.'

The laughter in his eyes belied the gravity of his tones, 'And you believed *me* one of them?'

Elinor's shoulders lifted. 'I respect the way you have immersed yourself in your tenants' problems. I wish I had more monetary help to offer.'

His reply was swift. 'You have all the qualities I want, my love. But what of you? Will you enjoy life in the country in such modest circumstances?'

She flinched. 'Please forget my early statements. I have regretted them many times.'

His kiss was rough. 'Do not make me wait too long for you, Elinor.'

They strolled on and Elinor asked, 'When did you know you loved me?'

'I cannot decide. Perhaps when you arrived on my doorstep like a waif to demand my protection.'

'You sounded angry at the time.'

'I was, or maybe I was more fearful than angry. I think I sensed that my freedom was slipping from me.'

'Christopher! You do not feel like that any more?'

His arm held her close to his side. 'I gave up my freedom of spirit to you long ago. My whole being yearns to make us indivisible.'

Elinor gave a contented sigh. 'I had no notion you could speak with such poetic sensibility.'

'I surprise myself,' he said modestly. 'And you, my dearest, have you loved me long?'

'I think from the beginning, though sometimes I hated you,' she said frankly.

'I deserved it! If my reasoning had not been so

confused I would have known you could not give your kisses lightly.'

She stopped to pull down his head to render further proof of her passion.

Christopher said gently, 'Do you think your papa would approve of me? Would he consider me a dull fellow to offer you a life in the country?'

'Dull!' Elinor laughed. 'If he saw you borrowing beyond your means to restore a decrepit manor and bring comfort to so many lives he would recognise it for the noble gesture, the *supreme* gamble, it is.'

Christopher's arm tightened about her slender form and they achieved a short distance before they found it necessary to reassure themselves that they belonged in truth, not merely in dreams.

Eventually they would arrive back at the manor. The walk would take an inordinate time, but every step would lead them nearer happiness and the promise of future ecstasy.

Masquerade brings you the age of romance

It was a time of wicked conspiracies and dastardly plots . . . of virtuous ladies abducted by the all-powerful lords of the nobility . . . vicious highwaymen and scheming villains . . .

It was an age of threatening intrigue and swashbuckling derring-do, when strength and swordplay were all that counted, and right and wrong were as nothing.

But, it was also a time of pure romance.

Masquerade
Romantic Novels of Long Ago

Masquerade romances are books
of love and adventure, suspense and intrigue,
set in times long past. Beautiful novels
that will sweep you away... to the colorful
world of Regency London... to the searing
passions of Czarist Russia... to the
tumultuous shores of Revolutionary France.

•

Many previously published titles are once
again available.
Choose from this exciting collection!

Masquerade

Choose from this list of early titles.

Relive a great love story...
Masquerade romances